Shaky Man

Shaky Man

Mark S. Parker

Illustrated by Marcia d. Crowder

 Pecan House Books

BROWN BOOKS KIDS

Shaky Man

Brown Books Kids
16250 Knoll Trail Drive, Suite 205
Dallas, Texas 75248
www.BrownBooksKids.com
(972) 381-0009

A New Era in Publishing™

ISBN 978-1-61254-862-3
Library of Congress Control Number 2015947426

Printed in the United States
10 9 8 7 6 5 4 3 2 1

For more information or to contact the author, please go to
www.MarkSParker.com

Shaky Man is dedicated to my father, Dr. Bobby E. Parker Sr. (1925–1999). He was the president of the University of Mary Hardin-Baylor in Belton, TX, for twenty years. Daddy was a lifelong educator, devoted to the advancement and enrichment of all. He was especially active in securing education for minorities, regardless of race, creed, color, or gender. He never met a stranger. He was my CoachDaddy. He leaned on many a ballpark fence.

Contents

Acknowledgments

With great gratitude I must thank as many of those who helped bring Shaky Man to the printed page as I can. Robyn Conley, the Book Doctor, was invaluable in her editing and suggestions in revisions. Thanks to all my friends at Brown Books who made this such a pleasant experience, especially Beth Robinson, Kathy Penny, and Derek Royal. And I cannot thank all of the early readers enough. There were too many to name here, and I know I would leave someone out if I tried. Their encouragement kept me going. A special thanks to Marcia d. Crowder for her wonderful illustrations. She captured Top and Mickey perfectly. Most of all, I have to thank my lovely wife, Ann. Without her love and support, none of this would have ever fallen into place.

Full Count

Ball three," called the umpire.

There I stood, facing a full count. I was starting to feel a little shaky with the game on the line. We (the Tonkaway All-Stars) found ourselves down four to three to the Oglesby All-Stars in the top of the sixth inning during this Division Championship game. I played first base. So did the manager's son, so I didn't get to play much. In the fourth inning, we'd sweated it out at three to nothing. Then, Skip Morrison made it to second base and Dub Elliot hit a home run, making it three to two. Somehow, Coach Blain in the first base coach's box, who had coached me for the John's Farm-acy team during the regular season, talked Coach

Roberts, the manager, into letting me pinch hit, since I batted left-handed and the Oglesby pitcher threw righty. I had a pretty good batting average during the regular season, with two home runs, although I wasn't really a long ball hitter. Both homers were at Optimist Field, which had a short fence. I hit for average, which was close to .400. Anyway, on my previous at-bat, I'd hit a home run, too. That had tied things up, three to three. Back-to-back homers, Dub and me. That rallied our fans. And I managed to stay in the game. Coach put me in right field.

From the batter's box, I heard my daddy down the right field fence line say, "Come on, Topper, you can do it, keep your eye on the ball."

CoachDaddy wouldn't sit in the stands with Mama. He was an old coach. Back then, he was teaching at Baylor. He always said the amateurs annoyed him. He liked to lean on the fence and chew on his cigar. Mama sat in the stands with Sis and yelled like crazy. "Come on, Topper." She was a couple of months pregnant. I couldn't wait for my little brother. He was due in early February.

I fouled the next pitch off to right field. It was a line drive that almost hit Coach Blaine. I thought he was going to catch it. He said, "Straighten it out, Top." Still full count.

Although my full name was Thomas Oliver Parsley, most people called me Top. My family called me Topper. Daddy's name was Bobby, not Robert, but most men called him Bob. Mama's name was Ruth, and eight-year-old little sister was Caroline. We just called her Sis.

Joe Ellis called me Topknot. I didn't much care for that guy at first. He was the biggest kid on our team and our best pitcher. He should have been biggest. His dad held him back in the first grade for football. Joe had pitched two nights earlier when we beat McGregor six to three and he wasn't eligible to pitch that night, so he played third base.

I fouled the next pitch down the left side. The Oglesby pitcher was huge. I'd have bet he shaved. Why was it that the biggest guys on All-Star teams were the pitchers?

Next pitch, I hit another foul ball behind the stands.

Tonkaway was a small town west of Waco. When we moved there from Brownwood in January 1967, Daddy didn't want to live in the big city of Waco. He preferred commuting to the Baylor campus, where he taught physical education classes, and let us live in a small town.

I liked small towns. We lived in Houston for two years while Daddy got his master's degree. We all hated it.

Tonkaway was just right. I hoped we would stay there until I graduated from high school. The people were friendly. Traffic wasn't as bad as Houston's. Plus, it was close to Nana's house in China Spring. Everyone loved it there. I was afraid that would change if I struck out in this game.

Another foul ball. I looked down at Coach Roberts in the third base box and got the "swing away" sign.

"OK!" I said to myself.

I liked to get out of the batter's box and lay my bat down and sprinkle dirt on the handle. Then I rubbed in the dirt real good and looked at the third base coach. I used a Nellie Fox thirty-two-inch bat. The fat handle felt natural. I choked all the way down to the nub. I heard the guy on W-A-C-O radio saying something about "little Tommy Parsley," stepping back into the box with a full count and down by one. Ouch!

No pressure there. Big, shaving righty from Oglesby brought the high, inside cheese. I couldn't resist. Swing and a miss. Game over. Oglesby went to Houston for the Area playoff. Tonkaway went home.

I looked down the right field line at Daddy. He just smiled. Daddy didn't get too worked up about stuff. I felt sick, though. Daddy turned and said something to the man he had been talking to throughout the game. He'd been leaning on the fence talking to someone I didn't expect. It was Shaky Man.

Anyway, for whatever reason, probably striking out, I didn't sleep very well that night.

Campout

Once baseball season was over, there wasn't a whole lot to do during the day except ride bikes and play down by the creek. Tonkaway Creek was heaven for a growing boy. We could wade, swim, and fish. People didn't mind if we used the creek behind their houses. The only place we kids didn't go was the creek behind Shaky Man's house. We were too scared. There was rumored to be a deep swimming and fishing hole right behind his place, but no one dared go near it.

One Friday night in August, Alan Carpenter invited the entire All-Star team to a campout in his backyard on Tonkaway Creek. He lived three doors down from Joe Ellis.

Most of the team showed up for the campout. We all brought sleeping bags. Mr. Carpenter grilled hamburgers, and Mrs. Carpenter made some homemade ice cream. She let us take turns turning the crank on the ice cream freezer. One of us would sit on the churn until our rear ends would get too cold to take it anymore, and then somebody else would take over.

After we finished eating, we played Wiffle ball until dark. We would have had to stop anyway because Joe finally cracked the ball. He'd been smacking the ball all evening. I thought everybody got tired of climbing over the Carpenters' chain link fence to fetch Joe's home runs. I wished he would have done that against Oglesby.

After dark, Mr. Carpenter helped us build a fire down by the creek, where we unrolled our sleeping bags. We roasted marshmallows, told jokes, and talked about the baseball season. Joe tried to pick on a couple of kids, but they just gave it back to him, so he clammed up.

I don't know how late we stayed up, but at some point, Jimmy McFarland said, "Anybody know any ghost stories?"

"I do, I do," said Rex Johnson, all excited.

"What's it about?" someone asked.

"The Green Fingernail," he said ominously.

"Do you promise it's scary?" asked another.

"Terrifying," said Rex.

"OK," we told him, "scare us."

"Well, see, there was this travelling toothbrush salesman who ran out of gas way out in the country one dark and stormy night. OK?"

We nodded, not sure about this.

"Well, see, there was this old, run-down, abandoned house nearby where he decided to run for cover until it quit raining. He went inside and found an old chair at the bottom of the staircase where he sat waiting. OK?"

We nodded.

"Well, see, then he heard a voice coming from up the stairs. OK?"

"What'd it say?" we asked.

"Guess what I can do with my Green Fingernail," Rex said in a deep voice.

He said it again; "Guess what I can do with my Green Fingernail? Well, the salesman couldn't go back to his car because it was raining too hard, so he just covered his ears, but it didn't help. The voice just got louder and louder, saying, 'Guess what I can do with my Green Fingernail.'"

Rex was standing up by then, saying it over and over in his deepest, scariest voice, "GUESS WHAT I CAN DO WITH MY GREEN FINGERNAIL!"

We couldn't stand it anymore and shouted back at Rex, "WHAT!"

"Well, see, that's just what the salesman said," Rex said with a real serious look on his face.

"So what could it do?" asked Joe.

Rex took his finger, twiddled his lips, and went "BWIBBITY-BWIBBITY-BWIBBITY."

We all rolled our eyes.

Joe said, "That was stupid."

At least Rex thought it was funny. He rolled in laughter on his sleeping bag.

I asked, "Does anyone know a real ghost story?"

Alan said, "I do, my dad told it to me. It's true."

"Is it about a fingernail?" asked Joe.

"No," answered Alan, "but it is green. The Green Ghost of Tonkaway Creek."

In the dark, somebody said, "That sounds scary enough, go for it."

Alan started his tale.

"There was an old pioneering family from Germany that lived on the banks of Tonkaway Creek in the early 1900s. They farmed the bottomlands and ran cows in the pastures. The farmer and his wife had three strong sons who worked on the farm with their father."

Skip Morrison blurted out, "I swear, if this farmer has a weird fingernail we're throwing you on the fire."

Everybody laughed except Alan. He went on without skipping a beat.

"The farmer started finding dead cows on his property. They weren't just dead, they were mutilated. He thought it must be a mountain lion. He knew there used to be bears in this country. Maybe it was a bear. When he and his sons started looking around for signs of whatever was killing the cows, they found the strangest tracks. Whatever it was had webbed feet with three toes, ten inches across, and walked on all fours. The killer was coming up from the creek. It could be tracked coming up and going out of the water. They couldn't imagine what it was."

Alan had our attention. It was apparent he wasn't joking, like Rex.

He continued, "The four of them sat down at the kitchen table that night to discuss what to do. Something had to be done about the slaughter. It was decided that, the next night, the three sons would spread out along the creek bed and wait for the animal or whatever it was coming out of the creek."

Alan picked up his flashlight and pointed it toward the creek. He said, "Sorry, I thought I heard a noise." Then he went on with the story.

"The next night, the three brothers took off down to the creek with nothing but their rifles, lanterns, an ax, and matches for a fire. They each had three cartridges for their rifles. The father waited on the back porch of the house. He could see down the hill as each son built a fire. They were each spread about a half a mile apart. Every once in a while, he could see the light of a lantern where one of the sons was walking around looking for something. Maybe they heard a noise or saw something move."

Feeling drawn into the story, I found myself sinking down deeper into my sleeping bag.

"The father could only wait and watch. He was holding his shotgun, just in case he needed it. His boys had made him promise not to come down to the creek, no matter what he saw or heard. They feared that he couldn't handle whatever they might face."

Alan was talking in a real soft voice by then. He was a good storyteller.

"Sometime around midnight, the father heard a gunshot and a terrible scream coming from the location of the fire to his right. The scream wasn't a mountain lion. It sounded human. The father watched as that son's fire went out and waited to see his lantern move toward his brother's camps. That didn't happen. The father decided the son let his lantern go out, too."

"What was it?" asked Rex. Rex's face looked white.

"Let me finish," said Alan.

"Not long after that, the father heard another gunshot and another scream, just like the first scream. This time, he was worried. This time, the fire didn't go out."

"He watched as the third son's fire went out and his lantern headed toward the middle son's camp. As the lantern approached the fire, he heard another scream. This time the scream was louder and more inhuman than before. It was followed by a very human scream. The father knew it was his son. There was nothing he could do. The noise had woken his wife and she moved behind him at the kitchen window. They both felt helpless as they watched the fire and lantern go out."

"What'd they do?" Hal Prasatik asked, big-eyed.

"Nothing," said Alan. "The father told his wife he could only wait for the sun to come up."

"At sunrise, the father saddled up his horse and wagon to ride down and see what had happened. He found the first son's mutilated body near what was left of the fire. The strange tracks were all around the campsite. He loaded his son's body in the wagon and followed the tracks to the middle fire."

"At the middle fire, he found the bodies of the other two sons. The third son was still alive, although the son was lying in a pool of blood with his stomach torn open. The father jumped off his horse and tried to stop the bleeding, but he was too late. The son died in his arms, but not before he could tell his father what had happened and what he saw."

"What was it? What happened?" We all wanted to know. Alan had us.

"When the last brother came up on the middle brother's camp, he expected that one of his brothers had killed whatever was slaughtering their cows. Instead, he saw a large, reptile-like creature clawing away at his dead brother's body. He fired all three of his bullets into the monster's back, but its skin was like an alligator's. The bullets didn't seem to faze the thing."

"The creature slowly raised up, turned around, and came toward the last brother. It walked like an ape and had one yellow eye. When the brother held his lantern up, the eye glowed like a cat's."

"The brother just stood there as the creature took a hunk out of his belly. As a last resort, the brother grabbed his ax and planted it in the monster's neck. That didn't kill it but stunned it enough that it stumbled backward and stepped into the fire. The brother watched as the reptile's clawed, webbed foot shriveled up to a nub. That's when it let out the most horrible scream."

"When the brother finished telling this story, he died in his father's arms. A few days later, after the sons were buried, the father went back down to the creek to look for tracks. Sure enough, for every three webbed tracks, there was one that was just a hole in the ground."

"Cows kept dying, and the old couple gave up on Central Texas. Some said they moved to California. Some said they went back to Germany."

"Wow, Alan, great story," Joe said, staring at the creek.

"Wait a minute," said Alan, "It's not over. I haven't gotten to the scary part."

He continued, "Some people say the creature is still out there. If you go down to the creek sometimes, you'll see tracks—webfoot, webfoot, webfoot, nub. Some people who go fishing or coon hunting or frog gigging at night sometimes report seeing a large yellow reflection in the woods. I know it sounds far-fetched, but that's what my dad told me."

It was getting late, and Alan's mom came down and told us it was time to go to sleep. We didn't want to let the fire go out, so if anybody woke up to go to the bathroom, they put some wood on it.

"Sleep tight, boys," said Alan, cheerily.

I didn't know about that. I could see Joe's eyes wide open every time I woke up during the night. One time I woke up and Paul Dodson was shining his flashlight into the woods across the creek. I wasn't sure whether he was hoping to see a reflection or not.

To tell the truth, I'm not sure how well I slept that night.

3

Morning

The sun came up too early for me. I think most of us stayed in our sleeping bags to stay warm. The fire had finally gone out. A few of the guys were walking down by the creek. They wouldn't admit it, but I was sure they were looking for webbed tracks in the mud. I didn't know what they would have done if they had found any.

Mrs. Carpenter brought breakfast down for all of us— bacon, scrambled eggs, biscuits, and orange juice. Hal said it was "larrupin'." We all laughed. That was a funny word.

While we were eating, the brave Joe Ellis said, "I hope none of you sissies bought any of Alan's baloney last night about that Green Ghost business. I knew from the start he was yanking our chains. I just didn't want to say anything and spoil it."

Alan just pursed his lips, shook his head, and said, "Believe what you want to."

Rex said, "If you're so smart, why don't you tell us a scary story? It doesn't have to be dark."

Joe said, "I don't have to make up some crazy story. I think y'all know what to be afraid of."

"What's that?" Rex asked.

"Well, if you're a kid in Tonkaway and don't know, you should know it's Shaky Man."

Most of the other boys nodded like they knew exactly what Joe was talking about. Rex just sighed. "You've told us before."

I'd heard a little bit about Shaky Man. I knew what he looked like. I'd seen kids in a group taunt him when he came to town. I remembered Daddy talking to him at the Oglesby game. I'd been so upset about striking out I forgot to ask Daddy about him.

Curious, I said, "Why don't you tell those of us who don't know much why we need to be scared?"

Joe replied, "OK, I hope you can keep your bacon and eggs down."

Joe continued, "I was sworn to secrecy on this, but I think all the kids in town need to know for their own safety. Number One: Shaky Man killed his wife and two young sons. This happened about twenty years ago. It's not clear where it happened. It may have been in Houston or Dallas. Some say it happened here in Tonkaway. Wherever it was, it was in all the papers."

"Why wasn't he put in jail?" I asked.

"He was arrested and put on trial," Joe said. "They let him go. He had some kind of alibi, and another guy was executed instead. The rumor was that he had some dirt on the judge and it wasn't a fair trial to begin with."

Rex said, "Now tell about Number Two, that's what we've really got to be worried about."

"I'm getting to that," Joe scowled.

"Number Two: He eats little kids."

"What," I exclaimed; "how do you know that?"

"You hang around long enough," answered Joe, "you'll see. Kids just disappear around here for no reason, and nobody says anything." He looked around at the group, "Y'all remember Priscilla Edwards, don't you?"

Heads nodded.

"She was the last to disappear. She was in the second grade."

"Why didn't her folks do something?" I asked.

"I was told it was because they had other kids they didn't want to lose. That's why nobody ever says anything about anything Shaky Man does. Supposedly, he has some mysterious power over the law in these parts and all the grown-ups know it."

"Wow." I was dumbfounded. "Please don't tell me there's a Number Three."

"Sorry," Joe said, "but there is. It's not quite as bad, but it's bad to me."

"So what is it?" Now it was like Joe and I were the only ones talking.

"He mistreats his dogs. He ties them up on real short chains with tight collars. He pretty much starves them. He feeds them crackers. Makes them drink rainwater. I was told they're just skin and bones."

"That's all hard to believe," I said.

"But you believed in the Green Ghost of Tonkaway Creek," Joe said, eyebrows raised.

"I didn't say that." He had a point. I did have a hard time sleeping.

About that time, Mr. Carpenter walked down to tell us it was time to roll up our sleeping bags and go home. Party over.

As we were leaving, Joe put his arm around me. "Now, Topknot, you can't repeat what I said about Shaky Man to anybody, especially your mom and dad."

"Why not?"

"Well, if they don't know about it, they won't believe you and they'll give you a scolding for saying such outrageous things. If they do know about it, they'll just deny everything, thinking they have to in order to protect you and your little sister. So just be careful."

Walking off, I turned around and said, "Joe, I have one more question about Shaky Man."

"OK, what is it?"

"Why does he shake like that?"

"That's easy," said Joe. "Guilt."

I told Alan and his parents thanks for a good time and headed home, walking real slowly. I was pretty sure I'd need a nap that afternoon. That was, if I could go to sleep.

4

Shaky Man

Folks had to see Shaky Man in person to fully understand. It's not that any kids saw him very often. He
would come to town to the grocery store and to pick
up old fence pickets and barn wood, supposedly for firewood.
No kids would go near him alone. After hearing Joe Ellis's
explanation, I understood why. Jane Ellen Phillips was the
exception. I'll tell about her later.

Needless to say, he scared the bejeezus out of us. He
wore a long, gray, wool overcoat, even in the summer. Nor-
mally, he appeared in town when school was in session so the
kids wouldn't tease him. Kids were brave in a group. They
would follow him down the street and mock him.

"Hey, Shaky Man," they'd yell, "where's your family?"

"Hey, Shaky Man, you hungry?"

"Hey, Shaky Man, why don't you let your dogs go?"

They followed so far behind, I'm not sure Shaky Man even heard them.

Joe would dare the little kids to go up and touch the Shaky Man.

Every once in a while, some brave soul would, then run away screaming. Not me. Not brave Joe Ellis.

Shaky Man lived deep in the woods above Tonkaway Creek. No one I knew had ever seen his house in the daylight. We just knew where it was and stayed as far away as possible.

Shaky Man shook. His hands tremored. His head bobbed up and down, right and left, like he was constantly answering questions. Sometimes, his head circled. It was weird. It was like he couldn't control it.

He was too shaky to shave right. He had crazy, old-man whiskers growing out of his cheeks, neck, ears, and nose. That, and his big, black glasses, made him all the scarier.

One night before school started, brave Joe came up with the bright idea that we should all go up to the Shaky Man's house and egg it. Egging was a big tradition in Tonkaway. Being new in town, I hadn't learned that yet.

A bunch of us boys and girls had ridden our skateboards around town and were sitting under the streetlight by the Milk Barn when Joe came up with his plan. Rex said he'd rather go inside and get a milkshake.

It didn't sound like a good idea to me, either, but I went along with it, being the new kid in town. I just hoped my folks didn't find out. Joe's older brother, Ralph, bought two dozen eggs and passed them out. We put them in our pockets and climbed into the back of Ralph's pickup. There were about eight of us. Ralph let us off at the cattle guard at the edge of Shaky Man's property. Ralph said he'd wait there, if it was OK with us. The coward.

We all walked slowly up the caliche road. I had never been more scared in my life. Joe acted brave, but I didn't believe it. When we reached the gate, there were three dogs waiting. They didn't bark and they weren't chained. They looked pretty healthy to me. Shiny coats and all.

Joe said, "Open the gate and let's go."

Sally Ellstrom opened the gate, and we crept up to the porch.

The house was dark. Joe said, "OK, cut loose."

All the other kids started throwing their eggs. I couldn't do it. Something wasn't right. Then a window broke and a light came on.

Everyone started running as fast as they could.

Joe screamed, "Hurry, before he eats us."

Joe had his eggs hidden inside his coat and hadn't thrown them all. He tripped going out the gate and smashed them inside his pockets. It was a mess. I kind of got a little kick out of that.

As we ran away, I heard a voice say, "Come on back, kids; that's OK. It was all in fun. You didn't mean any harm. I'll fix the window. Let me turn on the light."

When Ralph picked us all up, we couldn't get home fast enough.

Joe said, "You know why he wanted to turn on the light?"

We shook our heads.

"So he could see who was fat enough to eat!"

I didn't sleep very well that night, either.

Mickey

My folks quickly made friends no matter where we lived. It didn't take them long to hook up with the Paweleks, who lived down the street. They liked to sit in their backyard and visit with whoever happened to walk by in the evening. Mama and Daddy would take our lawn chairs to their house and sit in the backyard with them and just talk. Sis and I would go and play on their swing set and eavesdrop on the grown-ups.

Mr. and Mrs. Pawelek were a little older than Mama and Daddy, but they got along great. Their names were Raymond Sr. and Margie. They had four children, Raymond Jr., Paul, Nancy, and Susan. Everybody called Raymond Jr.

"Butch." Butch went to Baylor, and Susan, the youngest, was six, so the kids were really spread out in age.

Even though none of the Pawelek kids were my age, I still liked going down to their house to visit. I always felt welcome, and Mrs. Pawelek had cookies or candy to offer. They owned the second color TV I'd ever seen outside of a store. The first was at the State Fair of Texas, where I'd watched the *Ruff and Reddy* show. I would go to their house on Saturday nights to watch *NBC Saturday Night at the Movies* in color. There was always popcorn. It was a treat.

For some reason, Butch took a liking to me and would take me places. The first time I went hunting was when Butch took me rabbit hunting in the snow after Thanksgiving. I actually shot a rabbit, and Butch showed me how to skin it.

Butch would also take me with him to the Waco Boys' Club. He volunteered there while he was going to school. I had a great time. We played basketball, shuffleboard, football, soccer, and board games, and we also swam. During the Thanksgiving snowfall, they let us make sleds out of old highway road signs. We loaded on the bus and went to Cameron Park to sled down the hills. I'd never done anything like that before. At the Boys' Club, they learned to make do with what they had. I thought that was a good thing.

It was fun but an eye opening experience for me. For the first time in my life, I was playing games, swimming, and doing activities with boys whose skin wasn't white like mine.

Don't get me wrong. The N-word wasn't used in our house, but I'd heard it plenty. I'd heard it from prominent, churchgoing citizens. When Martin Luther King Jr. was in the news, I'd hear some people say things like, "That n***** is going to get it someday." He seemed OK to me. The world could get awfully confusing.

Anyway, prior to going to the Boys' Club, the only black people I'd really been around were maids and nannies. There were a few Hispanic kids in my school, but they were never in my class.

It was at the Boys' Club where I met, unexpectedly, one of the best friends I'd ever have. His name was Mickey Jackson and he was funny and he was black. Mickey could make me laugh just by smiling. When I saw his big white teeth, I knew he was fixing to tell me a big one.

"Hey, Top," he'd say. "Want to see me dunk?"

"You can't dunk," I smiled; "you're too short."

"Quarter says I can."

"I don't have a quarter."

"A dime'll do."

"OK." I wasn't sure I even had a dime, but I wanted to see what he was up to.

Mickey picked up the basketball and shouted to the gym, "Hey, everybody, watch this!" Then he dribbled up to the backboard and kept dribbling. He dribbled to the utility room and came out with a ladder. He set it up under the basket, climbed up, and dunked the ball. Mickey climbed down laughing.

I just shook my head and smiled.

"Where's my dime, sucker? You should have asked about the rules."

"What are the rules?"

"Ain't none." said Mickey, laughing, "Where's my dime?"

I dug deep and fished a dime out of my pocket. Lesson learned.

Mickey and I were almost inseparable when I went to the Boys' Club. I would tell Mama about all the stunts Mickey would pull and about his tall tales. She said she hoped to meet him someday.

When Butch took me to the club in the mornings, Mickey would take me home with him for lunch. He only lived two blocks away. His mother would come home from work and fix us sandwiches. She was a cleaning lady at the Mrs. Baird's plant and always had fresh, hot bread. She smelled like bread. Their house was small, but she did her best to keep it clean and make it home.

Mickey's father was a janitor at Baylor. I hardly ever saw him. He worked the night shift and was usually sleeping when I was there. Mickey talked about his dad all the time. He thought his Papa hung the moon. I was sure he was a great guy.

There was an unusually warm day right before Halloween that year. Mama saw the Paweleks in their backyard. She grabbed the lawn chairs, Daddy, Sis, and me, and we all went down the street to visit.

Sis and I were playing on the swings when Butch got home. He stopped and said something to his folks and Mama and Daddy. I noticed Mama had a quizzical look on her face. A little later, she called me over.

"Top," she said, "can you come here for a minute?"

She almost never called me Top.

"OK," I said, wondering what this was all about. "What is it, Mama?"

"Well," she asked, looking me straight in the eye, "you know your friend Mickey, from the Boys' Club?"

"Yes'm."

"Why didn't you ever tell me he was colored?"

"I don't know. I don't guess it ever came up."

That wasn't true, and I knew it. I never told her because I knew she would be OK with it, but I didn't know about other people, even members of our own family.

"Well, you could have told me." She was looking at me real hard right then.

My lip started to tremble, and my eyes started to water. I said, "Sorry, Mama."

"That's OK, honey. I'm sure Mickey's a real nice boy. Raymond Jr. says he is. Maybe he can come home with you someday."

By then I couldn't talk, and I turned around crying. Why? I'm not sure. Was I embarrassed? Ashamed? Was I worried about what people would think if I were seen walking down the streets of Tonkaway with a colored boy? Whatever the reason, my reaction made me feel mighty bad. Things sure got complicated for a sixth grader.

That night, when I said my prayers, I promised God I wouldn't be ashamed of my friends ever again. I didn't sleep great after that prayer, but better than I would have if I'd let things stew in my brain all night.

6

Jane Ellen Phillips

I said I'd tell more about Jane Ellen Phillips later, so here it is. Jane Ellen is Cherry Ann Phillips's little sister. Up to that point, Cherry Ann was probably my favorite person in Tonkaway. She was just enough tomboy to suit me and just enough girl. She was a lot of fun. Jane Ellen was different, though. Most of the kids called her "retarded." Mama told me that she was "special."

Special she was. She was the sweetest thing on this planet. She loved everybody she came in contact with. Even Shaky Man.

She also loved dogs. Any kind of dog.

When Shaky Man came to town and all of the kids were razzing him, Jane Ellen would run up to him and grab his hand and smile at him. When Shaky Man came out of the grocery, he always had a treat for Jane Ellen. It might have been a peppermint. It might have been some chocolate. He was always ready for her. They held hands and walked together for a block or two while the other kids harassed Shaky Man. They talked about something. No one ever got close enough to find out what.

Joe Ellis said that Shaky Man was just trying to fatten Jane Ellen up before he ate her.

One day in late November, Jane Ellen disappeared. No one could find her. The whole town was on the search. Cherry Ann was beside herself. She was frantic. She loved her little sister.

Before the night was over, the police, the sheriff's office, the constable, and everyone in Tonkaway were looking for Jane Ellen.

It was getting dark. I had an idea. Jane Ellen and dogs. I headed up to Shaky Man's house on the creek. When I got there, sure enough, there was Jane Ellen with those dogs with their shiny coats. She was cuddled up in the corner of the kennel with the dogs licking her. She was loving it.

"Jane Ellen, don't you know the whole town is looking for you?"

"Why?" she asked.

"Because you're missing."

She said, "I'm not missing, I know where I am."

"Well, your folks don't, and they're in a tizzy. Let's go to your house."

"OK," she said, reluctantly. "Shaky Man has the best dogs. I love them."

As we walked back to town, Jane Ellen held my hand and put her head on my arm. She was the sweetest thing in the world. She really was "special."

When we reached the Phillipses' house, there was great rejoicing. Mr. Phillips called the authorities and called off the search. Jane Ellen wouldn't quit talking about Shaky Man's dogs. I didn't think they were starving.

When I got home, I told Mama and Daddy all about my day. They said they were proud of me. I slept pretty well that night.

Joe Ellis

Joe Ellis called one day to see if I wanted to come over to his house and throw the football. Mama answered the phone. I heard her say, "Why sure, Joe; I know he'd love that. He'll be right over. He's just watching TV and needs to get out of the house."

Mama called to me in the den, "Honey, Joe called and wants you to come over and throw the football with him."

"But Mama, I'm watching TV."

"I think you've had enough TV for today," she said.

"But *Wild Kingdom* is on and Jim is in a pinch with a tiger."

"Go," she said, "now! Marlin Perkins always gets Jim out of his pinches. You know that."

"OK," I growled.

Off I went to Joe's, slowly. Mama knew I wasn't that crazy about Joe. She said that maybe I just needed to get to know him a little better. I guess that's why she told Joe I'd be right over. She could be very manipulative. I had just learned that word in English class.

Not only was Joe the biggest guy on our All-Star baseball team, he was the biggest guy on his Pop Warner football team. Was he an offensive lineman? No. Was he a defensive lineman? No. He was the fullback. I had been to their games, and Joe got the ball almost every other play. It looked to me like he was looking for some little kid on the other side to run over and stomp into the grass. He was pretty good at it, in fact. Joe scored a lot of touchdowns. I never saw one guy bring him down. I would have liked to have seen him go head-to-head with that big, shaving kid from Oglesby.

I wished I could have played Pop Warner football, but Daddy wouldn't let me. He said kids had no business playing football until they reached junior high because their bodies weren't ready. CoachDaddy said I could play in junior high, but only if I wanted to. He promised he would never push it on me and I should only play as long as I was having fun.

When I got to Joe's house, he was waiting for me in the front yard.

"What took so long?" he asked.

"I got here as soon as I could," I white-lied.

Joe said, "That's OK. I got to finish watching *Wild Kingdom*. Jim was in a pickle with a tiger, but Marlin got him out of it."

"Great," I mumbled.

"Let's go out back and throw," ordered Joe.

Out back was about an acre backing up to Tonkaway Creek. Mr. Ellis bought the place so Joe would have plenty of room to practice his punting and placekicking. I heard that Mr. Ellis made Joe run sprints back there, too. Joe was going to be Mr. Ellis's ticket out of town when Joe made the pros. Which sport didn't matter.

When we reached the backyard, Mr. Ellis was sitting at the picnic table on the patio, as usual, with a bottle of Jim Beam, as usual. He was a rough man. I never saw him wear anything except his work coveralls. As far as I ever knew, he came straight home from work every day, grabbed his bottle, and went to the picnic table to contemplate life and Tonkaway Creek.

Joe and I played catch for a while. Then he decided he wanted to play quarterback. He had me lining up and running routes—curls, cross routes, flag routes, and posts.

"Go long," he'd yell.

And I'd go long, real long. Joe could throw the ball a long way. I supposed he really did need an acre. He could throw it hard, too. Just like he threw a baseball. And he was accurate. On short routes, I thought he was going to knock a hole through me, he threw so hard.

From the porch, I could hear Mr. Ellis yelling at us, "Great throw, Joe." Or "Come on, Top, catch the ball, it was right in your hands." Stuff like that.

After a while, I was getting tired. Joe wasn't. I was doing all the running. Joe was just standing there throwing the ball. He threw me one that I bobbled and dropped.

Joe said, "Hey, Topknot, you look like Shaky Man."

Since I'd been searching for an excuse to take a breather, I walked the ball over to Joe and asked, "Is it true what you say about Shaky Man?"

Joe said, "What's true?"

"All that stuff about him killing his family and eating kids."

Joe said, "Of course, everyone knows it's true. The only reason nobody's turned him in is because they are afraid he'll eat their kids and he has power over the law. If you don't believe me, let's go ask my daddy."

I said, "I thought you told me to never talk to grown-ups about Shaky Man."

Joe laughed, "I know, but Daddy's pretty loose right now and I bet he'll talk. When he's like this, he starts talking and won't shut up."

That didn't sound like a very good idea to me, but we marched up to the porch anyway.

Joe said to Mr. Ellis, "Daddy, isn't it true what they say about Shaky Man?"

Through red eyes, Mr. Ellis said, "What, who?"

Joe said, "You know, the old guy who's so scary. The guy who eats kids and killed his wife and sons and nobody would turn him in. He's a cannibal and murderer, isn't he?"

"What in the world are you talking about?" Mr. Ellis raised his eyebrows at Joe as he lifted the bottle to his lips. "Where on earth did you get that?"

Joe answered, "From Gerald Dawson."

"Gerald Dawson, huh? Gerald Dawson ain't nuthin' but a ducktailed, leather-jacketed thug. Why on earth would you listen to anything that hoodlum had to say?"

Joe said, "But Daddy, if Gerald said it, I have to believe it."

"Why?" said Mr. Ellis. "Have you been spreading this nonsense around to your friends?"

"Well, Daddy, I thought I should let them know when they were in danger."

"What danger?"

"Of getting eaten. Like Priscilla Edwards."

Mr. Ellis said he'd never heard of Priscilla Edwards and held his head in his hands for a long time. I thought he was trying to think through the Jim Beam. When he straightened up, he reached in the pocket of his coveralls and pulled out a five-inch Buck knife. It appeared to me that Mr. Ellis wasn't as loose as Joe had thought he was.

Mr. Ellis said, "Here, Joe-Boy, go out front and cut me a nice switch off the peach tree and trim it up. I don't talk to people much, but I'd never repeat anything Gerald Dawson told me and I want to make sure you don't, either."

Mr. Ellis opened the knife and handed it to Joe, handle first. He said, "You're lucky I'm in a good mood. When you come back through the house, why don't you change out of those shorts and into some jeans? That'll make it easier."

"Yes, Daddy," Joe said as he turned. He had tears in his eyes. I felt sorry for him. I knew what was coming.

Mr. Ellis slurred, "Top, you'd better run home now. Joe and I need to have a little talk."

"Yessir," I said.

When I got home, I was real quiet. I kept thinking about Joe and the whipping he was going to get. I turned on the TV. Mama asked me what was wrong. I said, "Nothing." She was too savvy for that. By the time supper was over, she had drug the whole story out of me, except I still didn't tell them all of the things Joe said about Shaky Man. She was furious. Daddy wanted to go over and whip Mr. Ellis. After dessert, everybody took a deep breath and things calmed down. I couldn't quit thinking about Joe.

When I went to bed, Mama came in my room. She sat on the side of my bed and asked me, "How do you feel about Joe now?"

"Differently. He can't help being what he is."

Mama said, "Can I make a suggestion?"

"Sure."

She said, "When you say your prayers tonight, pray for Joe and pray for Mr. Ellis."

"Mr. Ellis?"

"Yes, Mr. Ellis needs prayers, too, probably more than Joe."

Well, I said those prayers, and it felt pretty good. I hoped it helped. I still didn't sleep very well that night.

Spin the Bottle

After Thanksgiving, I was sent to John's Farm-acy to pick up some dog food. John's was where everyone in Tonkaway went for supplies. They went to Piggly-Wiggly for groceries, but John's was the go-to place for any other supplies, even hardware.

On my way, I passed by the Phillipses' house. Cherry Ann was out front riding her skateboard. I waved at her.

She said, "Where are you going?"

I said, "To John's, I'll talk to you on my way back. OK?"

She said, "OK."

When I got to the Farm-acy I picked up a big bag of Ralston-Purina Puppy Chow for our Boston terrier, Buster.

Buster was barely a puppy, but Mama still bought him Puppy Chow.

Buster was a mess. Mama and Daddy got him for me because I didn't want to leave Brownwood. That was my reward for moving to Tonkaway—a crazy dog. Daddy said he would settle down as he got older. That couldn't come soon enough. Buster would jump on anybody and anything. He was wild.

Anyway, as I was in line to check out with the dog food, I noticed that Shaky Man was in line in front of me. He was buying dog food, too. That was unusual for somebody who starved his dogs. After I checked out, I found myself following Shaky Man up the street.

When he approached the Phillipses' house, Jane Ellen came running out and grabbed his hand. Shaky Man reached in his pocket and handed something to Jane Ellen. It looked like they were having a conversation.

As I reached the Phillipses' driveway, Cherry Ann skateboarded out to me and asked, "Are you going to Sandy Warnke's birthday party tonight?"

I said, "I guess."

Sandy Warnke was in our class. She was what Daddy would call a "fast girl." She dated seventh graders. I liked her well enough. She was nice to me. She was nice to all the boys.

Cherry Ann said, "I'm going, but I don't know what to expect."

"What do you mean?"

"I don't know," she said. "I just know Sandy and her close friends."

"Well," I said, "I'm still new around here, so I'll just have to watch and learn."

Cherry Ann and I watched Jane Ellen and Shaky Man walk up the road.

"Cherry Ann," I asked, "what do you think about that?"

"What?" She answered.

"Your sister and Shaky Man. Aren't you afraid of him and for her?"

"I don't know what to think. Jane Ellen has an innocent soul. She loves everybody. Even Shaky Man. He hasn't hurt her. I know what everybody has heard, and I don't know what to believe."

I said, "Joe says Shaky Man is just trying to fatten Jane Ellen up before he eats her."

"I say Joe Ellis is a buffoon. That's putting it nice."

"What about Priscilla Edwards disappearing? Gerald Dawson says Shaky Man ate her."

Cherry Ann shook her head and rolled her eyes.

"Priscilla Edwards was a foster child. She was adopted by a family out of Fort Worth. It all happened real fast. Gerald Dawson! Ugh! I never heard that nonsense. Gerald Dawson and Ralph Ellis are what keep me from going to the Milk Barn at night."

About that time, Jane Ellen came skipping back to the house with a big smile on her face and a little chocolate on her lips. She gave me a great, big hug. She was the sweetest thing in the world. I went on home to feed Buster, the monster dog.

That night, I walked over to Sandy's house for her twelfth birthday party. It seemed like a thirteen party. I was still eleven. My birthday wasn't until January.

Mary Lou Garry was there. She was Sandy's best friend. Mary Lou was going steady with an eighth grader from Waco. Talk about fast. She had his ring around her neck. Mary Lou's sister, Brenda, was helping with the party. Brenda was in the eighth grade, too.

When I walked in, they were listening to the new Monkees album. "Daydream Believer" was playing. It had been all over the radio. I was already tired of it.

I tried to stay close to Cherry Ann because I was more comfortable around her. Joe was there, as were Rex, Alan, Hal, and most of the guys from baseball. Sandy liked popular folks. I didn't consider myself especially popular; I was just the new boy who played sports.

After we ate hot dogs and potato chips, Mrs. Warnke brought out the birthday cake. It was pink with a Barbie-in-a-sports-car decoration. Barbie's hair was blowing back. Fast.

When the cake was gone, Mrs. Warnke said, "How about a game?"

We all said, "OK!"

Mary Lou and Sandy said, "Spin the bottle, spin the bottle!" So we played spin the bottle.

If you don't know about spin the bottle, it's where all the boys and girls get in a circle; usually, the girls are on one side of the circle and the boys are on the other side. Somebody spins a bottle until it points to a boy and a girl. Then they have to go somewhere and kiss.

Mrs. Warnke was all for that. She finished her Dr. Pepper and put the bottle in the middle of the living room floor. We all circled around.

The first couple to line up was Rex and Julie Williams. I thought Mrs. Warnke had this all planned out because she was sitting in the middle of the floor, spinning the bottle. When a couple lined up, she sent them to the big living room closet to smooch. Julie came out smiling. Rex looked like he'd kissed a fish.

Joe and Mary Lou were next. That was an interesting pair. Joe went in all puffy and came out white knuckled. Mary Lou was indifferent, as always. She was used to kissing seventh graders, after all.

This wasn't going very well with me. Here I was in a new town, getting to know everybody and playing a game I really didn't like. I looked over at Cherry Ann, and she looked like she wanted to be someplace else, too.

The next couple was Kitty Parsons and Alan. Kitty was in the fifth grade, but she and Sandy were good friends. She seemed like she was too young for a party like this, much less to be playing spin the bottle. When they came out of the closet, I thought Alan was going to pass out. Apparently, Kitty was a little more aggressive than I expected.

I felt like my luck was running out. I wasn't ready for all of this. I got up from the circle and went to the den and told Mr. Warnke that I wasn't feeling well and was going to walk home. It was just a block away. He called my folks to tell them to be looking for me.

On the way home, I sure was glad the bottle never stopped on me. If it would have, I would have hoped that the girl was Cherry Ann. We could have just gone in the closet, told a joke or two, and come out smiling like we were the best kissers in the world. But I didn't want to take any chances.

When I got home, Mama asked why the party ended so early. I told her it was a school night. I slept pretty well. Better than I would have if I'd have had to do any kissing. I wasn't ready for all that. I couldn't help but keep from thinking about Alan's overwhelmed face. I made plans to stay away from Kitty. That was for sure.

Stay-Over

Right after Christmas, Mama insisted I bring Mickey home for the weekend. She wanted to get to know this boy I talked about all the time. Christmas Day was on a Monday that year. Butch took me to the Boys' Club on Wednesday, and I asked Mickey if he wanted to spend the weekend with us. School would still be out, so he could stay until Monday, New Year's Day. He said he'd have to check with his mom, but he was sure it would be OK.

Friday after lunch, Daddy and I picked up Mickey at his house. Mama wanted him to be sure to bring his church clothes. Mrs. Jackson liked that.

It was early in the afternoon, and Daddy wanted to take us to the Orpheum Theater to see *The War Wagon* with John Wayne. Unfortunately for Daddy, it sold out. We had to see *The Jungle Book* instead. A bunch of little kids were crammed in there. Mickey and I pretended to be disappointed about not seeing John Wayne, but there had been a lot of good talk about the Disney movie. Mickey and I both liked the animals in *Jungle Book*. I think even Daddy liked the movie a little bit. He said, "That was no John Wayne film, but it was funny."

On the way to Tonkaway, Mickey kept singing "The Bare Necessities." He liked the part where Baloo sang about picking a pawpaw or a prickly pear and getting a raw paw.

When Mickey reached the line that said, "Next time beware," he'd look at me sideways with his eyes opened wide and point at me with his index fingers.

Daddy would look in the rear view mirror and grin.

Mickey Jackson was undoubtedly the happiest guy I knew.

On Saturday morning, we hurried into the kitchen for breakfast. Mama stood at the stove, and Daddy sat at the table, reading the newspaper and drinking his coffee. I saw Sis in the living room, watching cartoons.

It didn't take Mickey long to start teasing Sis. He'd say, "Oh, Caroliiiiine. Wudja' bring me summo' pancakes?"

She'd laugh and play like she hated being called Caroline. Nobody called her that but Nana. Then she'd get him some more pancakes. I warned Mama that he could eat.

After breakfast, Mama told me, "Why don't you go show Mickey around town?"

"OK, that won't take long. Maybe we'll run into some kids at the park or something."

We put on our jackets and walked the neighborhood streets toward town. Pretty soon we were in front of the Phillipses' house, and Jane Ellen was playing by herself out front. She came running out to say hi.

"Hi, Jane Ellen. How're you? This is Mickey."

Jane Ellen looked Mickey over real good. Up and down. Then she pointed at him. She told him, "You're colored!"

Mickey smiled. Then he took on a serious appearance. He looked Jane Ellen over real good. Up and down. Walked around her. He gave her a good going over. Then he pointed at her. He told her, "You're white!"

Jane Ellen laughed and jumped up and down. She said, "I like you." Then she ran up and hugged Mickey's leg.

I told him, "Don't get the big head. She likes everybody."

Cherry Ann came out to say hello and met Mickey. We talked a while and then headed on our way. I decided we should work our way toward the creek and let Mickey see the Tonkaway version of the Brazos River.

We walked past the Carpenters' house, but they weren't home. I'd hoped Alan might be around to tell Mickey about the Green Ghost of Tonkaway Creek. Mickey said that was all right. He didn't like ghost stories anyway.

Staying along the creek bank, we came up behind the Ellises' house. They weren't home, either, so we kept walking. When we reached a certain point, I told Mickey we had to turn around.

He asked me, "Why?"

"Because we're getting close to Shaky Man's place," I answered.

"Shaky Man? Who's that?"

I told him all that I had heard about Shaky Man as we walked back up the creek. I told him I didn't know how much of it was true, but I just knew all the kids in town were afraid of the man. I told him about egging his house and how I didn't think his dogs looked all that bad.

Mickey said, "OK, let me get this straight. This old man lives up there by himself with dogs he abuses."

"Right."

"And he killed his family."

"So they say."

"And he eats kids."

"According to what I've been told."

"And he just gets away with it."

"That's it."

Mickey said, "I think we should go back and go up to his house and knock on the door."

I said, "What! Are you nuts?"

"I mean it. We need to find out."

"Find out what?"

"Find out whether he likes white meat or dark!"

Mickey laughed, pushed me, and took off running. I didn't even try to catch up. I was laughing too hard.

I yelled at him, "You're sick!"

That night our whole family headed to the Paweleks' to watch *Saturday Night at the Movies* in color. Mickey had never really watched a color TV. *African Queen* turned out to be a good movie with Humphrey Bogart and Katherine Hepburn. We all agreed we could have done without the part with the leeches.

Sunday morning, I was in the bathroom getting ready for church. I could hear Mickey in the dining room.

"Oh, Caroliiiiine. Wudja' bring me summo' bacon?"

"Hush up, you," Sis laughed.

By the time I hurried into the kitchen, she held another plate of bacon.

Mickey asked Daddy if he could see the funny papers. He liked to read *Dick Tracy*. I did, too. We had a lot in common.

Everybody at church went out of their way to be extra nice to Mickey. Some folks said it was good to meet my "colored friend." Mickey told me he liked our church, but it was a lot different from his. He said we sure were quiet, even though we were both Baptists.

When we got home, Mama had a pot roast in the oven. Nana came over and joined us for Sunday dinner. You should have seen Mickey put away the pot roast, mashed potatoes, gravy, and green beans. We started out with half a loaf of Mrs. Baird's bread on the table, but it disappeared. Mama made peach cobbler for dessert.

Mama said, "My cobbler's never as good as yours, Mother."

Nana said, "Did you sprinkle water on the dough?"

"You never told me to do that."

"You never asked me."

I looked at Daddy. Daddy looked at me. We'd heard this conversation a million times before.

After we finished eating, Mickey and I changed clothes and settled down in front of our plain old black-and-white TV to watch the Harley Berg wildlife show on KWTX. Harley Berg had a pen full of rattlesnakes, and one escaped. We laughed at how the cameraman followed that snake around the studio until somebody caught it and flung it back in the pen. Harley Berg didn't want any part of that snake.

Then Harley Berg told the story about seeing a fox on a riverbank with a stick in its mouth backing into the water. As the fox backed into the river, fleas started gathering on the stick. The fox kept going into the river until he was up to his nose. Then he let go of the stick. The stick was covered with fleas. And that's how a fox gets rid of fleas!

I'd heard that story before, but I still liked it. The show closed in the usual manner. I was surprised when Mickey recited the ending with me.

Harley Berg always closed with these words: "Amigos! Grande y chiquitos! Und grosse kleinen und fraulein. Big and little friends. Let's keep'em swimmin', runnin' and flyin'. And support your wildlife boys, 'cause they's your buddies."

Mickey and I sure had a lot more in common than most folks would think. As soon as the show was over, the phone rang. Mama answered.

"Hi, Joe," I heard her say, "Sure, he'd like to come over. He has a friend from Waco staying with him. Sure, they'll both be right over."

I said, "Mama, *Wild Kingdom's* coming on."

She said, "I don't care. I don't want Mickey to go home tomorrow and tell his mother that he sat around and watched TV all weekend."

Mickey smiled and said, "Oh, Caroliiiiine, wudja' get-memuh jacket?"

Sis said, "Hush up, you," as she went for his jacket.

Walking to Joe's house, I warned Mickey that we'd probably have to let Joe play quarterback while we did all the running. Mickey said he didn't mind. He liked to run.

Joe was waiting for us in his front yard. I introduced him to Mickey, and they shook hands like big boys. We moved around back where Mr. Ellis sat at the picnic table with his bottle, as usual. I introduced Mickey. Mr. Ellis said, "Hi," in a low voice and didn't accept Mickey's offer to shake. He just stared down at the creek.

Joe said, "Y'all come on. Let's play catch."

"Now you'll see what Joe means by playing catch," I whispered to Mickey.

Joe had us running the usual routes. Then he decided we should take turns playing defense. I couldn't cover Mickey. He was too slippery and fast. He had Joe laughing. Mickey made some great catches. He would catch the ball and do a somersault, coming up with the ball in the air.

"I should have told you what an athlete he is," I said to Joe. "I guess you've figured that out by now."

"Yeah, he's pretty good."

When it was my turn to play receiver, I didn't have a chance then, either. Mickey stuck close to me, having a big old time making me look bad. I didn't mind because I knew he couldn't help being so talented.

The whole time we played, Mr. Ellis sat at the picnic table and glared at us. He never said anything like "Good catch" or "Good throw." He was real solemn.

After a while, I said, "Aren't you guys getting tired?"

Mickey said, "Heck, no, I'm having fun."

Joe said, "I'll play as long as y'all want to. Daddy says I need the practice. Mickey makes a good target."

Just then Mr. Ellis yelled down, "Joe, come up here a second."

"I'll be right back," said Joe.

Joe went up, and Mr. Ellis hissed in his face about something. I figured Mr. Ellis's whiskey breath was burning Joe's eyes just then. Finally, Joe came back down to where we waited for him.

He said, "I guess y'all need to leave. Daddy wants me to go in the house now."

"OK," I said. "See you later."

As we walked off, Mickey turned around and waved, saying, "Thanks, Joe, it was fun. Nice to meet you and your dad."

Mr. Ellis stared from the porch—not a good stare. I was glad to be leaving.

On the way home, we passed Alan Carpenter's house. He was outside, so we talked to him for a minute. I told him that Mickey needed to hear about the Green Ghost. Alan said it wasn't the right time. It needed to be told in the dark with flashlights. Mickey said that was just fine with him. He could wait until next time. Or longer.

Since it was New Year's Eve, we were allowed to stay up and watch Johnny Carson. Then we saw the ball drop on Times Square.

Before we went to bed, for some reason, I apologized to Mickey. I said, "I'm sorry about taking you over to Joe's. I didn't know Mr. Ellis was going to act like that."

Mickey said, "That's OK. Doesn't bother me. I still had fun."

"How can it not bother you? It would keep me up at night."

"If I let stuff like that get to me, I'd never go to sleep. Welcome to my world. Don't you worry about it. I don't. My papa taught me not to let other folks put their malfunctions on me. You shouldn't, either."

I went to sleep thinking about that. No malfunctions. Sounded good. I slept OK.

10

Little Brother

It was the middle of January, and my little brother was due in about two weeks. I'd had a bad cold and gone to the Tonkaway Clinic to see Dr. Gillespie. He gave me a shot and some pills. While I was in his office, he just wanted to talk about football. Like everybody else in town, he was a big Tonkaway Tiger fan. He was a Baylor Bear fan, too. He wanted to know what Daddy thought about next season, the new quarterback, and anything else he could think to ask. When I hopped off the exam table, he told me not to have a relapse because he would be out of town for about a week visiting his son in Houston.

I hoped he would be back in time to deliver our baby. Every Tonkaway kid I knew had been delivered by Dr. Gillespie in that clinic.

I ran into Joe on the way home. He wanted to know why I hadn't been to basketball practice. I told him I'd been sick and hadn't been to school, either. He didn't care about that.

"Have you seen Shaky Man lately?" he asked.

"No, it's been a while," I answered. "Why?"

"No particular reason. I had to go apologize to him, you know."

"How'd that go?"

"OK, I guess. He didn't get mad or anything. In fact, he didn't say much. Daddy made me shake his hand, and we left. That was about it."

After leaving Joe, I went straight home. Mama's car was in the driveway, and Daddy was driving up. When we got in the house, I looked in the kitchen and asked, "Where's Mama?" Daddy didn't know. He told me to find her.

I started looking around the house, saying, "Mama?" It was strange that she hadn't picked Sis up at Nana's house. The bedroom door was open so I went in. The bathroom door was closed.

I called, "Mama? Mama?" No answer. The door was unlocked, so I tried to open it. It would barely budge. The light was on, and I could open the door enough to see Mama in the mirror on the floor, lying up against the door.

I hollered, "Daddy, come quick; something's wrong with Mama."

When Daddy saw what I saw, he kept saying, "Oh my gosh. Ruth, wake up. Oh my gosh. Ruth, wake up."

Daddy was able to open the door and lay Mama down on the floor. She was in a pool of water. Daddy said her water broke and she passed out. He said she never did have a very strong stomach for bodily fluids.

Daddy said, "Topper, quick, go get the doctor!"

I said, "But I can't, Dr. Gillespie's out of town."

"No, the other doctor."

"What other doctor?"

"Dr. Boone. Tell him we'll meet him at the clinic."

"Who's Dr. Boone?"

"Shaky Man! Now hurry!"

I never ran so fast in my life—all the way in the dark to the house on Tonkaway Creek.

When I reached his front door, I knocked as hard as I could. I didn't know whether Shaky Man, I mean Dr. Boone, was hard of hearing or not. I'd never talked to him. Jane Ellen was the only kid I knew who had.

When he came to the door, I breathlessly explained everything that had happened as best as I could. About how Mama's water broke and she passed out in the bathroom and they were going to meet us at the clinic. All the while, Dr. Boone was getting dressed as fast as he could.

When he was ready, we took off down the road. He could move pretty well for his age, which I couldn't even guess.

When we were close to the clinic, I said, "I didn't know you were a doctor."

He just replied, "For forty years—now all I do is fill in for Dr. Gillespie when he's out of town."

When we arrived at the clinic, Mama and Daddy were waiting in the car. Dr. Boone waved at them and went straight to unlock the clinic door. Once inside, he headed for the delivery room to wash up. Sticking his head out the door, he said, "Bob, bring her on in. Nurse Hale will be here any minute, and we'll get started. You and Top can wait in the waiting room. There's a phone in the receptionist's office if you need to call anybody."

Nurse Hale showed up soon after that, and Daddy and I went to the phone so he could call Nana. He told her what was going on and that Sis would have to spend the night with her. The house was unlocked, so they could go over and pick up a change of clothes for school tomorrow.

Just as I expected, it wasn't thirty minutes before Nana and Sis showed up at the door.

"We figured we could wait here with you just as well as at home," Nana said.

We waited what seemed like a long time. After a while, I told Daddy I was going to get a drink of water. He said, "Take Sis with you."

On the way, we passed the delivery room. We could hear Mama making some awfully unpleasant noises. Sis and I looked at each other. I knew what she was thinking, because it was the same thing I was thinking. We crept up to the delivery room door and cracked it open. Just a little bit. Just enough to see.

What we saw inside was nothing short of a miracle. Dr. Boone was as cool as a cucumber. He wasn't shaking at all. It was like he was a different person. He was talking to Mama very calmly, telling her to push, that it wouldn't be long.

Sis and I went back to join Daddy and Nana before we got caught peeking. I was so surprised I had forgotten about getting a drink. We climbed up on the couch to wait. It wouldn't be long.

I don't know how long we slept. It could have been a few minutes. It could have been a few hours. When Daddy woke us up, he said, "Come see your new baby."

My little brother was in a room with Mama and Nana. They were all smiles. Somebody had messed up and dressed my brother in pink. I guessed the clinic was out of boys' clothes. He was pink, too, and tiny. Mama was holding him.

"What's his name?" I asked.

Everyone laughed. "Sorry, son, this is your new sister," said Daddy.

I just said, "Oh."

After I let that sink in, I thought I'd better ask, "OK, what's her name?"

Mama said, proudly, "Samantha. Samantha Marie. Isn't that pretty?"

"I guess so."

Then I asked, "Where's Dr. Boone?"

Daddy said, "He's gone home. He'll be back in the morning to check on Mama and the baby. Nurse Hale is going to spend the rest of the night with Mama and the baby. You and Sis need to kiss Mama and Nana goodnight and get in the car. We're going home. You still have school tomorrow."

Lying in bed that night, I figured I'd better get used to having two sisters and give up on having a brother any time soon.

Samantha Marie. Maybe I'd call her Sammy. Maybe I'd teach her to play catch. Maybe this wouldn't be so bad. I slept pretty well after that.

My Birdhouse

Mama and Sammy came home from the clinic after a couple of days. Dr. Boone came by to check on them every day. I was usually in school and didn't see him. When Dr. Gillespie returned to town, he started checking in on them.

Sammy was coming along real well. When she was born, she weighed five pounds, six ounces. Mama said Sis and I were bigger than that, but we weren't two weeks early, either. Mama also said Sammy had a good appetite. Daddy said that meant she liked to "belly up to the trough."

Two weeks after coming home, Mama made Dr. Boone a pecan pie and asked me to take it to him. It was a warm Saturday afternoon for February. The pie was also still warm as I started up the road to Tonkaway Creek. I wished Mama had made a pecan pie for us. She said her pies were never as good as Nana's. You could have fooled me.

I had never seen Dr. Boone's house in the daylight. Wondering what it looked like, I made the turn up his gravel road. As I approached the cattle guard, I started noticing a lot of birds and hearing a lot of birds singing. That was strange. There weren't that many birds in town. As I got closer to the house, I saw more and more birds.

When I reached the front yard, I couldn't believe it. There were birdhouses everywhere. Some were plain. Some were kind of elaborate, the three-story variety. Some were painted. Some were rustic. I started looking around at them and forgot about the pie.

Dr. Boone must have seen me out of his window. He came outside and said, "I see you've discovered my little hobby."

"So this is what you do with those fence pickets," I said. "I was told you used them for firewood."

"Why would I need to haul firewood out here when I have so many trees?" he laughed. "I'm always on the lookout for old fence pickets and barn wood. They make great birdhouse material."

"Did you make all of these?"

"Sure did. I'm about to run out of room, though. I don't know what I'm going to do with them." Then he asked, "What are you holding?"

"Oh, I almost forgot." A little embarrassed, I told him it was a pecan pie from Mama as a show of thanks for what he had done that night at the clinic and the days after.

He said, "She didn't have to do that, but I'll take it. The best thing about it is that I got some company today. That doesn't happen very often, especially with youngsters. Let's take that pie inside, and I'll show you my shop, if you're interested in that sort of thing."

"Sure," I said. I'd never seen a real woodshop.

Out in the backyard, there was a big barn with a large pile of firewood stacked up in front. Dr. Boone slid the big door open and invited me inside.

Once inside, Dr. Boone turned the lights on. His shop had more tools than I'd ever seen in a workshop. Circular saws, table saws, and hand saws. Carving tools, hand drills, and a drill press. There were tools I had never seen before but he would later teach me how to use. My daddy could do a lot of things, but I wouldn't say he was exactly a handyman. A hammer and a screwdriver were about the extent of his toolbox.

Dr. Boone asked, "Do you want a tour or are you in a hurry?"

"Oh, no, no hurry." I was fascinated.

He showed me his table saw, miter saw, and drill press, just to name a few. He had hand tools that he said people didn't use much anymore, like a drawknife.

"Have you been doing this your whole life?" I asked.

"No, just the last fifteen years or so."

"What made you start?"

He answered slowly, "Well, that's a long story. Maybe I'll tell you someday, but not right now. How would you like to make your mother a birdhouse?"

"I'd love it!"

If I hadn't seen him so steady in the delivery room, I wouldn't have thought it was possible for the former Shaky Man to operate and handle tools and create anything requiring precision. Once we started on my birdhouse, it was the same way.

He pulled some fence pickets from a stack and set them by what he called a radial arm saw. He showed me how to measure and mark the pieces. Then he showed me how to cut the boards without taking a finger off with them. When he measured and marked and cut, he was as steady as any man. The rest of the time, he was as shaky as ever. Maybe that was another long story he would tell me someday.

He showed me how to nail the pieces together. Then we used the drill press to drill a hole in the front for the birds to get in and a little hole for a perch.

After I had glued a short piece of dowel in the perch hole, Dr. Boone said, "That should do it for now. Your mother is probably wondering where you are. Bring the birdhouse back and I'll let you paint it."

"I sure will."

Off I went down the road, carrying my birdhouse by the baling wire we had attached to the top to hang it by. When I reached the front yard gate, I knew I'd forgotten my manners. I turned around. Dr. Boone was still on the porch, watching me leave.

"Thanks for everything," I waved.

He waved to me. "Come back."

When I walked through the front door of our house, I went straight to the kitchen table and proudly placed my birdhouse there.

"Mama, come see what I made you," I shouted.

Coming from the back room, she said, "Why, Topper, that's beautiful. You made that?"

"Dr. Boone taught me how. You should see all of his bird-houses and his shop. They're pretty impressive."

"So that's where you've been all this time. I figured you were at Joe's house letting him play quarterback."

Joe Ellis. I did need to go see him and tell him what a dope Gerald Dawson was for saying such bad things about such a nice man. I felt bad enough for believing it all after we moved to town. Then I knew that Jane Ellen was smarter than people gave her credit for being.

That evening at supper, I couldn't quit talking about the doctor. Dr. Boone this. Dr. Boone that. Mama and Daddy just let me talk. Mama said it was too bad he was running out of room for his birdhouses. She thought maybe he could start selling them. I thought he might be too shy. Daddy said he thought there was a lot to Dr. Boone that we didn't know about. I just knew that I couldn't wait to go back and paint my birdhouse.

Then I remembered to ask Daddy what he and Dr. Boone had been talking about that night at the Oglesby game.

Daddy said, "Just baseball. He's a big baseball fan. That's not the first one of your games he's gone to. You just never noticed him. He knows all the players. He follows the big leagues, the minor leagues, Little League, any kind of baseball. He just loves the game. I'll bet he can quote every statistic there is."

Since I had a lot to think about, I laid awake for a while that night. Life sure could get complicated for a sixth grader. I thought grown-ups made it that way. Once I got to sleep, I slept like a log.

12

End Times

As soon as I could, I took my birdhouse back to Dr. Boone's to paint it. He said he was glad to see me. His painted birdhouses were really neat. Some looked like farmhouses, with chickens and eggs. He had one for Halloween. It had a witch in the window, goblins, jack-o'-lanterns, bats, straw, and corn stalks. Mama would have loved one of those.

I decided to paint mine so it looked like a house with songbirds. It had a red roof, yellow siding, windows with curtains, front and back doors, red birds, blue birds, robins, and hummingbirds. I'll admit it was a copy of one of Dr. Boone's, but he didn't mind.

As I painted, I let things troubling me go through my twelve-year-old mind. There had been a three-night revival at the First Baptist Church the previous week. The preacher had talked a lot about the end of the world. Rex and Hal went down front to get saved. I had been baptized in Brownwood when I was eight because Scott Brunner got baptized. That wasn't a very good reason, but I wanted to cover my bases. I was kind of worried and had been thinking about it. Life sure was complicated.

To make matters worse, our class went on a field trip to the Civil Defense Center in Waco the same week as the revival. We got to try out the crackers we would eat when the Russians bombed America. Then we went back to school and had a drill where we went out in the hall and put our backs against the wall and our heads between our legs. I didn't know what good that would do against atomic bombs.

With all of that on my mind, I started thinking about church camp from a couple of years earlier. I'd gone to a Lutheran camp near Fort Worth with a friend of mine in the summer after the fourth grade. It was a nice camp with horseback riding, canoeing, and lots of activities. We had campfire services every night.

On a Wednesday, the camp counselors had the bright idea that they would pull a funny prank on all the kids. They warned us that some inmates from a nearby insane asylum had escaped and were on the loose. We should be careful and stay close to our cabins and the headquarters.

That night at supper, we could hear what sounded like gunshots in the distance. The campfire service was short and sweet and ended with a warning to go straight to our cabins.

Around midnight, we heard all kinds of yelling and screaming. The male counselors were running around in blue jeans and T-shirts between the boys' and girls' cabins. They had ketchup on their faces and shirts so it looked like blood. Everything happened so fast we were scared plenty. We had our flashlights, and they were going in every direction. After a minute or two, the counselors turned on the lights and everybody had a good laugh. Sort of. My heart wouldn't quit racing.

It turned out that the gunshots we heard was one of the counselors cracking a bullwhip in the woods to fool us.

Things got serious the last night of camp. Everyone who wasn't saved was invited to throw a stick on the fire to show they wanted to give their life to Christ. One boy from another cabin got up and told his story after throwing his stick in. It seemed he was all caught up in the insane asylum joke and hid his pocketknife under his pillow that night. When the counselors came in, all crazy-acting, the boy said he came six inches from stabbing one of the counselors in the throat before realizing who it was. That scared him to death, and it bothered him a lot, so he wanted to turn his life over to Jesus. That confused me more for some reason.

Then I started thinking about a Wednesday night at Training Union at church when I found an illustrated book of the Bible. It was a long, wide volume of the whole Bible. The artwork was very good. I made the mistake of looking in the back at the Book of Revelation. Talk about scary! There were drawings of all kinds of demons and monsters and desolation. I got chills and put the book back on the shelf.

The whole religion thing was bothersome to me.

All of these things tumbled around my brain as I painted.

Dr. Boone moved toward me and hovered over my shoulder. "Looks good, Top."

"Not as good as yours, but Mama will like it."

"I'm sure she will," he nodded, shaking a little.

For some unknown reason I asked, "Dr. Boone, do you ever think about the end?"

"The end of what?"

"Time. The world. I don't know. I hear people talk about the end all the time, especially preachers, and I hear bad things on the news."

"Well, Top, I'm not a very good one to ask about those things. I don't get out much because of my condition. I don't have a TV. I do read the newspaper. But I'm in my seventies now, and I don't worry about those things anymore. Besides, my world ended thirty years ago, and it's never been the same."

"What do you mean?" I asked.

"Top," he said, "I think I'm going to tell you something that no one in town other that Dr. Gillespie knows. And that's just because you're a good ball player and painter."

I blinked a couple of times, trying to decide if I should thank him or let him keep talking. He continued talking before I could respond.

"Before I retired to Tonkaway, I spent almost forty years as a forensic specialist at the Medical Center in Houston. I spent my days with cadavers and testifying in court. It was very satisfying work. I felt like a detective. They should make a TV show out of it. Or I should write a book. Late one night, I was on duty for a case when all of the available doctors were called in on an emergency. There had been a terrible automobile accident, and the emergency room was short-handed. A man, a woman, and two children had been brought in. They were all injured, quite severely. It turned out that I was the most experienced doctor available. The rest were mostly interns. The first thing we needed to do was to triage the victims."

"What's triage?" I asked.

"That's where you have to decide who is most likely to survive with or without treatment, who could survive with treatment, and who likely won't survive even with treatment. You treat those who could survive with treatment first. That came from French doctors in World War I."

"Oh," I nodded, kind of sad for the ones who wouldn't get treatment.

"The woman was beyond saving. The nurses put her on life support, but it was hopeless. She died soon after arrival. The man had minor injuries and was released the next day. There was hope for the two boys. They both had internal injuries. I had to perform the operations. I stayed with them for the days before they died. There was nothing else I could do. They were my sons. The woman was my wife. It was a coincidence that I was on duty that night."

"What about the man who ran into them; what happened to him? Was he drinking or something?"

He said, "We'll never know. He was a big-time District Judge in Harris County. No charges were ever filed."

"Gee, Dr. Boone, I'm sorry." I'd stopped painting.

"That's OK. Do you see why my world ended?"

"I guess. This religion stuff gets over my head," I said.

"Mine, too," he sighed. "I'll tell you what I learned through all of that—the hard way. God was there."

"What does that mean?"

"It's simple. I tried to make it complicated for a long time. I tried drinking for a while. That didn't work. I tried working long hours for a while. That didn't work. One day I just realized that God had been with me all along and I didn't know it."

"Where was he?" I was awfully interested in what he was saying.

"Right here, son," smiled the doctor. "He was never very far. He was with me in family and friends. Kind strangers. Good work. Opportunities to give outside myself. He was always there, just like the Bible says. I just didn't know it. Now I do."

That was a lot for me to take on at once. I appreciated what Dr. Boone said, but I had to think about it.

I finished painting my birdhouse, told the doctor thanks again, and headed home. My little head was full of conflicting thoughts. There was one certainty I knew for sure: I liked Dr. Boone more and more all the time.

Earlier that day, I had asked him, "Dr. Boone, who's your favorite team?"

"The Baltimore Orioles, of course."

It had to be a bird. I should have known.

Mama loved the birdhouse and had Daddy hang it on the patio.

I lay awake that night thinking about life, religion, and art. That was a lot to think about. I probably slept well, knowing God was there.

Headlines

Once basketball season ended and before baseball practice started up, I began going to Dr. Boone's after school. My folks were pretty happy about it, knowing my whereabouts for a change.

That happened in late April of 1968. The doctor let me work on his birdhouses, sometimes painting, sometimes cutting pieces out of old fence pickets, and sometimes nailing boards together he had cut.

"Top, you're getting pretty handy around the shop."

I liked the compliment, but Dr. Boone had some strict shop rules. For one, I had to sweep up before I left. For another, every tool had to go back where it belonged. I was afraid that, if I didn't do those things, he wouldn't let me go back.

At that point in time, I felt like I knew Dr. Boone well enough to ask the big question.

"Dr. Boone," I took a deep breath, "why do you shake?"

He chuckled. "Top, I get my tremor from my grandfather. It's hereditary. I've been to see neurological specialists, but there's not a treatment yet. I'm sure there'll be one someday. Someday there'll be a pill for everything."

"I see," I said.

Changing the subject, I told him, "Don't you think we need to find a way to start selling your birdhouses? Mama thinks they would be popular with bird lovers. You've run out of places to hang them, and they're piling up in the corner."

He said, "I don't know how I could do that. I wouldn't want to open up a store, but I have to keep making them for my own good."

"You could sell them at the Memorial Day Craft Fair at the City Park," I said.

"No. That's not for me. I'm not comfortable around people, and people aren't comfortable around me. My shaking makes others 'shaky,' if you will."

"How about Mama and I sell them? She'd love that."

"That would be fine with me. What would you call them?"

I thought a minute. What would Mickey come up with? I said, "How about 'Bird Housecalls by Doctor Boone'?"

He said, "Where did you come up with that so fast? You have a quick mind. That's pretty good."

"I have another idea, since we're making so many birdhouses."

"What's that?" Dr. Boone was steady and smiling.

I liked it when he was that way. He could calm himself down when he wanted to, or when he had to. I'd seen that.

"You could advertise in the paper."

"I wouldn't even know what to ask for these things," he said.

I told him, "Mama thinks you could sell these painted birdhouses for eight or nine dollars, easy."

"Top," he said, "if I could sell these silly things for that much, I'd come out of retirement, hire you and all your friends, and make a killing. I'm willing to give it a try if you and your Mama are."

"We'd love it." I was excited that he was willing. I thought this might go somewhere.

Then Dr. Boone changed the subject.

"Top, while you're here, would you run out to the mailbox and get my newspaper?"

"Sure," I said.

I went to the mailbox and came back with the paper. I kept painting another Halloween birdhouse as the doctor opened up the *Waco News-Tribune*, reading on a workbench.

A couple of minutes, later the doctor said, "This is horrible. This sort of thing doesn't happen in Central Texas. It happens in Houston or Dallas, but not in Waco."

"What happened?" I asked.

He said, "Look at this headline." Then he turned the front page toward me. It said in big bold letters:

BAYLOR PROFESSOR MURDERED ON CAMPUS

JANITOR HELD ON SUSPICION

I asked, "Who was it?" I thought it might be somebody Daddy knew.

"A philosophy professor named Jefferson Farquar," he answered.

Then I asked, "Who did it?"

He said, "They arrested a custodian named Leonard Jackson. They say he stabbed the professor in the back and neck numerous times. They're going to wait on the autopsy."

"LEONARD JACKSON!" I shouted, "That's Mickey's dad. There's no way he could have done that. I've only met him a couple of times, but Mickey's my best friend. There's no way. There's just no way."

"Now, settle down, Top. I've been through a lot of these things in my career. You never know until it's over."

"But Mickey's such a good guy. His dad can't be a killer." I was protesting. I wanted to see Mickey. I wanted to talk to Mickey.

"Top," said the doctor, "there's not much you can do right now. Let's just clean up and let you go home and tell your folks, if they don't already know."

I started sweeping, and the doctor started putting up tools. His brow was furrowed. He said, "You know, that name, Leonard Jackson, rings a bell with me. I'm going to have to think about that. I know that name from somewhere."

When I was finished, I went home. Mama and Daddy were waiting for me. They had seen the news on TV about Mickey's papa. They knew I would be upset.

We ate supper, and Daddy gave me a long talk about the judicial system and fairness in society.

I said, "But, Daddy, he's colored and accused of killing a white man. I know I'm just a kid, but I worry about those things. I've heard people talk down about coloreds."

Daddy said, "We can only hope for the best. You go get ready for bed now."

Bed was the last thing I was thinking about. I was thinking about Mickey, Mrs. Jackson, and Mr. Jackson. What were they going to do? The next day was Saturday, and I was going to see if Butch would take me to the Boys' Club.

Sleeping wasn't much that night.

14

Waco

When I woke up the next morning, Daddy was already in the kitchen drinking coffee and reading the morning paper. He said there were more details about the murder.

"Did you know this Dr. Farquar?" I asked.

"I knew who he was," said Daddy. "He didn't have a very good reputation with the students and faculty. Apparently, he was kind of hard to get along with. His office was in Pat Neff Hall, so I never ran into him."

Daddy officed in the Marrs-McLean building. That's where he taught his PE courses. I loved hanging out in the gym there. I could shoot baskets all day.

"What does it say about Mr. Jackson?"

"The police say he was found holding the body with a bloody knife in his hand. He claimed he was coming to clean the office and found Dr. Farquar and was trying to help him."

"Who called the police?"

"Nobody knows. That seems to be a mystery. Mr. Jackson says he caught a glimpse of a small person going down the stairs when he got off the elevator. He couldn't tell if it was a man or a woman. That's all he knew before he walked in the office. It doesn't sound good."

"What else?"

"The report shows that Mr. Jackson's fingerprints were found all over the room and all of the desk drawers were open."

I told Daddy about how I wanted to go see Mickey, and he understood. He said if Butch wasn't going to the Boys' Club, he would take me.

After breakfast, I walked down to the Paweleks' house. They were all sitting around their kitchen table talking about the news. Butch wasn't surprised when I showed up. He was already planning to go to Waco.

When we reached the Boys' Club, we asked about Mickey. Mr. Garza, the director, said Mickey hadn't been seen for a couple of days. Since he lived only two blocks away, I asked if it would be OK if I walked down to Mickey's house. Butch and Mr. Garza both said that would be fine. Butch told me to be back by three. That's when he needed to go home.

Mrs. Jackson answered the door when I reached the house.

"Why, Top," she said, "what a surprise. Come on in. Mickey will be so glad to see you."

Mickey was sitting on the couch watching the noon *Farm Report* with Johnny Watkins. He wasn't smiling. I think that was the first time I'd seen him without a smile. I guess he was glad to see me, but he didn't get too excited about it.

"Why are you watching that?" I asked.

"Nothin' else on," he said. "Besides, I'm not really watching anyway."

"What are you doing then?"

"Just thinking about Papa."

"Want to go for a walk?"

"Where to?"

"I don't know. We could walk down by the river. Have you had lunch?"

He said, "I haven't much felt like eating."

"Mrs. Jackson," I called to the kitchen, "is it OK if Mickey and I go for a walk and get something to eat? My Daddy gave me some lunch money. It's enough for both of us."

She said, "Well, I could fix you something, but you boys do what you want to."

We left the house and walked up Herring toward Cameron Park and the Brazos River. Mickey wasn't saying much.

When we reached the park, he said, "You don't believe my papa did it, do you?"

"Of course not," I said, "the paper just doesn't make it sound too good."

"I know. All that stuff about fingerprints and the knife and drawers open. Not good for a black man."

"Maybe he'll get a good lawyer," I said, trying to be positive.

"We can't afford a good lawyer," said Mickey. "Mom's already trying to figure out how we'll get by while Papa's in jail. She'll either have to work extra hours at Mrs. Baird's or get another job."

Just then, a car passed us and we got an ugly stare from the driver. A white boy and black boy walking together down the street apparently wasn't a welcomed sight. I probably wouldn't have even noticed that before becoming friends with Mickey.

We didn't say any more until we reached the river. I could tell Mickey's brain was going in all directions.

He said, "You know, the fingerprint thing, it just makes sense. Papa probably cleans that office two or three times a week. And I'm sure he empties the trash every day. His fingerprints are probably all over the Baylor campus."

"Maybe you should be his lawyer," I said and gave him a little push.

He kind of smiled. That was good to see. I sure wanted to see the old Mickey. We both needed a laugh.

We followed the river down to Franklin Avenue and walked out to the middle of the bridge over the Brazos and leaned on the rail.

After a while, I said quietly without looking at him, "Hey, Mickey, you know what runs but never walks?"

He turned to me and said, "I dunno, what?"

"A river."

I thought he was going to hit me. Instead, he kept shoving me and shoving me until he was hugging me. I didn't know if he was laughing or crying.

Finally, he said, "That was stupid."

"I know, but you laughed. It wasn't any stupider than some of the things you've said."

"That's a matter of opinion."

I said, "I'm hungry; do you want to go to Clark's and get a cheeseburger?"

"I'm not sure they'll let me in," he replied.

"That's OK; we'll eat outside."

Clark's Drive-In was on Speight Street. They had great burgers. I went inside and ordered while Mickey waited at one of the picnic tables outside. I ordered two cheeseburger baskets and two Dr. Peppers.

While I was waiting for our order, I could hear a couple of men in one of the booths talking about the killing in the news.

One of them said, "Yeah, that n*****'ll be lucky to get out of jail alive."

The other one said, "You're right about that. When was the last time you heard about a lynching?" He laughed.

"It's been at least fifty years since Waco's seen one that I know of, but you never know when people are going to get stirred up," said the other man.

I was sure glad Mickey didn't hear that. I expected a lot more talk like that before the trial was over.

It didn't take us long to eat. Mickey must have been starving. I guess he was feeling better. He could have eaten two cheeseburgers.

On the way back to his house, Mickey kind of loosened up a little bit and acted like his old self. He started teasing me about my hair and clothes and PF Flyers. He said, "Who do you think you are? Johnny Quest?" I liked that.

We sure were tired when we got back. I suppose we walked at least five miles. I told Mrs. Jackson that I would see her and Mickey again real soon. She thanked me for coming. Mickey smiled and said, "Bye, Top, thanks."

I got back to the Boys' Club right at three as Butch was leaving. I needed to get home, too, for baseball practice. I told Butch all about the Jacksons and the problems they were going to have making it with Mr. Jackson not working. Butch said he would ask around at Baylor and see if there might be some way to help them out. I thought Daddy might be able to talk to somebody, too.

That night at supper, Mama and Daddy wanted to know everything, so I told them. Mama said Mickey could come stay with us after school was out if that would help. I doubted he would leave his mom alone.

When I told them about the car driver and the men at the drive-in, Daddy just shook his head.

He said, "This old world has a long way to go. We think we're good people, but we're not quite there yet. I hope you remember this."

"Don't worry. It'll be kind of hard to forget."

"Just know one thing. Most people are good. It's the few knuckleheads who make the noise. That's who you'll hear from. Not the good ones."

I can't really say how I slept that night. I felt better having seen Mickey, though.

Memorial Day

May of 1968 lasted forever. If it weren't for baseball and birdhouses, I'd have gone nuts. Mr. Jackson's trial kept being delayed for reasons I didn't understand, so he stayed in jail. Mickey spent the weekends at our house. He didn't get to play baseball that season. His mom didn't think it would be a good idea. Too many distractions, she said. He came to all the John's Farm-acy games he could so he could tell me what I was doing wrong. As if having a CoachDaddy wasn't bad enough.

Despite anything my two sideline advisors said, I played pretty well that season. I had already hit five home runs and batted cleanup for John's. I guess it helped not being the new boy anymore.

The only game we had lost up to that point was to Barbie's Bar-B-Q on opening day. We didn't score a run. It was four to zip. Rex Johnson's dad had thrown batting practice to us at every practice, and he only threw fastballs. He believed if you could hit a fastball, you could hit anything. We found out otherwise. The hard way.

Michael Brady came out throwing for Barbie's, and all he could throw was junk. Soft junk. He had us swinging out of our shoes. It's a wonder nobody threw their backs out. I did get one dribbler back to the mound. That may have been the closest thing to a hit we had. CoachDaddy kept saying, "Wait on it, Topper. Be patient." That was easy for him to say. By the time that game was over, I longed for some nice, fast, high cheese. At least that didn't look quite so bad when I missed.

We knew the real reason Mickey didn't play ball that year was that Mrs. Jackson was afraid. They were getting a lot of hate mail and threats over the phone. The police had to watch their house and follow her to Mrs. Baird's and back. Mickey's neighbors took turns walking him to school. Those were also reasons why Mrs. Jackson was glad to have Mickey spend his weekends in Tonkaway with us, to get him away from all that.

When we had a Friday night game, Mickey would spend half the game in the stands with Mama and the girls and half the game down the fence line with CoachDaddy and Dr. Boone.

Cherry Ann brought Jane Ellen to our games. They sat in the stands close to Mama. The problem with Jane Ellen was she wouldn't sit still. She was all over the place, especially when Mickey was around. Jane Ellen loved it when Mickey teased her.

School let out on the Friday before Memorial Day, which was the next Thursday. All of the big festivities were held on that holiday, including the Craft Fair.

Just as we promised, Mama, Daddy, Mickey, and I set up to sell the doctor's surplus birdhouses at the fair. Daddy rented a tent. Mama made signs that said:

BIRDHOUSE CALLS
HANDCRAFTED BY
DR. WALTER BOONE

Below that, Mama painted a black doctor's bag with a bluebird and a red bird perched on top. Mama was pretty artistic.

Daddy, Mickey, and I brought a carload of birdhouses from Dr. Boone's barn, and Mama hung them all around the tent. They looked great. The doctor came by early to see how things looked, but he said he couldn't stay. We didn't expect him to. He also said another carload waited if we needed it.

Once the fair opened, business boomed. A lot of people wanted birdhouses. The Halloween version sold out really fast. Daddy said we weren't asking enough for them. I thought he just didn't want to have to go get any more.

Mickey and I stood out front and helped ladies carry their birdhouses to their cars. It gave us something to do. Mama did all the selling.

Around lunchtime, I saw Joe Ellis show up with his mom and dad. They were down the row from our tent, looking around at all the other tents and eating Frito pies. Joe waved and started walking toward us, but his daddy grabbed him by his belt loop and pulled him back. Then he held Joe's chin to his face and started telling him something sternly. I don't know what he was saying, but they soon turned and went the other direction. We didn't see them again.

Soon after that, Mama sent us to pick up another load of birdhouses. The doctor couldn't believe it when we told him how well it was going.

When we got back to the fair, there were three rough-looking men in the parking lot who watched us start unloading. They especially had an eye on Mickey. Even I could see that. Daddy told Mickey to stay at the tent with Mama and that he and I would finish unloading. Mickey looked confused but didn't ask questions.

Later on, those men came walking through the fair, stopping people and talking to them. They would point at our tent and shake their heads. We saw them stop the Baptist preacher and his wife. They listened a minute, then walked away while one of the men was still talking and came straight to our tent.

Mrs. Bailey said, "Ruth, I love these birdhouses. I want two."

Mr. Bailey said, "Bobby, can I talk to you a minute?"

They walked off a little ways, under a tree, and visited for more than a minute. It was quite a while. The whole time, Mrs. Bailey and Mama talked about the weather and what a nice turnout the fair had. Mrs. Bailey paid extra special attention to Mickey. She told him what a handsome young man he was and how glad she was to see him.

After they finished their visit, Daddy came back to the tent and said, "Honey, I'll be back in a little bit. Brother Bailey is going to stay and help a while. It turns out that he's real interested in birdhouses."

Daddy left in the car. The rough men kept stopping people. It may have been my imagination, but it seemed like business had really slowed down. With Daddy gone, the men would just stare at us. Mama told us to not pay them any attention.

Daddy came back in about fifteen minutes. He didn't say much except to thank the Baileys for staying around.

Pretty soon, another car pulled up in the parking lot. It was the sheriff. He got out of his car all smiles.

Sheriff Holder started going up our row of tents, stopping to talk to everybody he met. Shaking hands, patting backs, rubbing shoulders. You would have thought it was an election year. He walked by our tent and waved, "Hi, Bob. Hi, Ruth. Hi, Top. Hi, Mickey. How's business? Sure like those birdhouses. I'll have to get one for Martha on my way out."

He worked his way down the row until he reached the rough men. Still smiling. We couldn't hear what was said, but Sheriff Holder reached out and shook their hands and patted their backs. Pointed to the sky. Pointed down. He pointed to the parking lot a couple times. Then he shook their hands again and kept walking, shaking hands and patting backs as he went.

The men just stood there and talked to each other. The sheriff came back, and Mama gave him one of the birdhouses that looked like a barn.

"Martha will like this one," she said.

Sheriff Holder thanked her, took the birdhouse to his car, put it in the back seat, fished a toothpick out of the front seat, placed it between his teeth, and leaned against the front of his car. Arms crossed, all smiles.

It wasn't long before the men started leaving, staring on their way to the parking lot. We were glad to see them go. The sheriff drove off with a wave and a smile.

Besides all that, it had been a great day. There were only two birdhouses left, and Mama wanted to keep those for Christmas presents. Mickey and I ran up to the doctor's house to tell him the good news.

He said, "I'll have to put you boys to work for real now. No more goofing off."

That night, I asked Daddy about the men while Mickey was in the shower. There were things we didn't talk about around Mickey.

Daddy said, "They were just some out-of-town riff-raff trying to stir up trouble. To tell you the truth, Joe's daddy bothered me more than those guys."

"How did those men know Mickey was here?" I asked.

"I suppose the Knucklehead Club has its own news network."

Mickey jumped out of the bathroom just then, announcing, "Time for *Star Trek*, Vulcans." It was Thursday night.

After watching *Star Trek,* we went back to my room to get ready for bed. We just talked about stuff. If anything was bothering Mickey, he wasn't letting on.

When we went to bed, he said, "Live long and prosper."

"Live long and prosper, brother," I smiled.

For some reason, I always slept well when Mickey was in the house.

16

The Trial

June brought sweltering temperatures to Central Texas. Waco set a record for over thirty days over 100 degrees with no rain. Baseball practices were brutal.

A lot had happened since the killing, with what happened to Robert Kennedy and Dr. King, Viet Nam, race riots, the Cold War, and all the other bad stuff on the *Huntley-Brinkley Report*. On top of all that, it seemed like a lot of white people in Central Texas couldn't wait for Mr. Jackson to go to the electric chair. I'd heard some men talking outside John's Farm-acy laughing about "that n***** goin' to see Ol' Sparky." I was glad Mickey wasn't with me, but I was sure he'd heard plenty of it. I had to keep reminding myself about what Daddy had said about the "few knuckleheads."

All I wanted to do was play baseball and make birdhouses. That took my mind off all the other things going on around town.

The trial lasted two weeks. It felt like two years. Mama, Daddy, and I went to Waco every day. My folks wanted to be there to support Mr. Jackson. That didn't make them very popular around town, but they didn't care. I went over to keep Mickey company. Nana kept Sis and Sammy.

Most days, we went to the Boys' Club or to Cameron Park. Sometimes, we'd just play catch or sit on the porch. Later in the afternoon, we'd walk over to the courthouse and wait for Mama and Daddy to come out so we could get the latest report. We were too young to go inside the courtroom.

On the next-to-last day, we couldn't stand it. Ball and gloves in hand, we went to the courthouse to wait. We knew that final testimonies would be heard. Daddy thought closing arguments might begin. Daddy wouldn't say so, but I could tell he was worried.

When we reached the courthouse, we were surprised to see Joe Ellis out front with his glove bouncing a baseball off the side of the building.

"What are you doing here?" I asked.

"Daddy wanted to come over and see what all the hubbub was about. My mother was working, so he had to bring me with him."

"Why'd you bring your glove if you weren't going to have anybody to play catch with?" Mickey asked.

"I have to wear my glove everywhere I go for a week. I missed a pop-up in a game the other night and Daddy went bonkers. Now I even have to sleep with it. Did you ever try eating wearing a baseball glove?"

Sometimes, it was hard not to feel a little sorry for Joe.

Mickey said, "Let's play three-way."

We formed a triangle and started tossing the ball around. None of us were too focused on what we were doing. After a while, we decided to just sit on the courthouse steps and wait.

So we sat there not saying a word, heads down. I was blindly tossing the ball up and down. Suddenly, the ball didn't come down.

I heard a familiar voice say, "Thanks, Top, that's just what I was looking for."

We turned around, and there was Dr. Boone, except it hardly looked like Dr. Boone. He was wearing a nice gray suit, had a haircut and a good shave. He was shaky, but not too bad.

"What are you doing here?" we all asked.

"I have an appointment with Mickey's father's attorney. Can I keep this ball for a little bit?"

"Sure," I said, puzzled.

"You boys come in with me. You might learn something."

We all looked at each other and told him, "We can't go in; we're too young."

He said, "I know the bailiff. I'll get you in."

We followed him up the steps and through the big doors. At the entry to the courtroom, Dr. Boone opened the door and motioned to the man guarding it.

He said, "Charlie, you don't mind if these boys come in for a little civics lesson, do you? They'll stand at the back and not say a word. I promise." He looked at us. "Isn't that right, boys?"

We all nodded. "Yes, sir."

"OK," said Charlie, and we all went inside.

The courtroom was packed. From what I could tell, Mr. Jackson's lawyer was asking somebody questions about something. People whispered everywhere. I could see Mickey's mom sitting behind Mr. Jackson. Mama and Daddy were sitting behind her.

Mr. Jackson's lead attorney was a Mr. Dulany. He had been appointed by the court since the Jackson's couldn't afford a high-dollar lawyer. Daddy had told me that Mr. Dulany had done a good job of showing that Mickey's papa's fingerprints should have been all over Dr. Farquar's office since he was in there cleaning several times a week. The bloody knife and open drawers were the big problems.

After Mr. Dulany finished questioning the witness, the judge called for a short break. Dr. Boone walked down the aisle and whispered to the attorney, handing him my baseball. That was peculiar. I knew this had to be hard on the doctor. He had a tough time around crowds. Dr. Boone sat down next to my parents.

When the judge came back into the courtroom, the bailiff said, "All rise."

Everyone stood up, the judge came in, tapped his gavel, and said, "Mr. Dulany, do you have anyone else you would like to call in defense of Mr. Jackson?"

Mr. Dulany said, "Yes, your honor, but, before I call the next expert witness, I would like to ask for a demonstration of an important physical characteristic of Mr. Jackson's."

He held up my baseball.

The prosecutor stood up and objected loudly.

The judge tapped his gavel, "Will Mr. Jackson be testifying?"

"No, your honor. Just throwing me this ball."

"This is highly unusual, but proceed. If it proves to be unrelated, I will have it stricken from the record."

Mr. Dulany turned, handed the ball to Mr. Jackson, and asked him to stand. He then stepped about ten feet away and said, "Mr. Jackson, please toss me that baseball, softly, overhand, if you will."

Mr. Jackson did just as he was asked.

Mr. Dulany caught the ball and turned to the judge, saying, "Your honor, please let the record show that Mr. Jackson throws with his left hand. You can sit down now, Mr. Jackson."

The judge said, "So be it." Or something like that. I couldn't really hear for all the bustling. The jury was stone-faced. I had been watching them the whole time. You would have thought those twelve white men were playing poker.

"Thank you, your honor," said Mr. Dulany, speaking loudly. "Now I'd like to call the final defense witness."

The judge tapped his gavel to quiet the courtroom.

"Proceed," he said.

"I'd like to call Dr. Walter H. Boone to the stand."

The doctor stood up. He wasn't shaking at all. He was just as calm as he was the night Sammy was born. He went to the stand and swore to tell the truth, the whole truth, and nothing but the truth. And that was before God.

"Can you give the judge and the jury your credentials to testify in this matter?" asked Mr. Dulany.

"Yes, I received my medical degree from the University of Alabama in 1928. I was a forensics specialist at the Houston Medical Center for over forty years."

"So you have worked closely with the Houston Police Department on cases such as this?"

"Yes, sir. And I have testified in over a thousand murder cases in my career."

"Did you have an opportunity to examine Dr. Farquar's body while it was in the morgue?"

"Yes, I did, at your request and with the court's permission."

"Can you please share with the judge and the jury your findings?"

"Yes, it is my opinion that Dr. Farquar died of multiple stab wounds all coming from his back, right side. The fatal blow was likely to the carotid artery in his neck. I counted eleven wounds in all. I filed a complete report for the record."

"Did you develop an opinion about the perpetrator in the process of the examination?"

"Yes," said the doctor. "It's all in my report. I believe the murderer was much shorter than Dr. Farquar, right-handed, and not very strong."

"Why do you believe the perpetrator in this case was not very strong?"

"Because most of the stab wounds were only one or two inches deep. I think the neck wound probably came first and the victim became unconscious and died soon after that. The other wounds were not that critical."

The prosecution objected, but the judge let the doctor proceed.

"The blade of the murder weapon was six inches long, and a man as strong as Mr. Jackson would have thrust it to the hilt every time."

Another objection. "Speculation," said the prosecution.

The judge overruled.

"And why, Dr. Boone," asked Mr. Dulany, "do you think the murderer was shorter than Dr. Farquar?"

"Dr. Farquar was six foot and one inches tall. All of the stab wounds were on an upward or level trajectory. The fatal blow to the neck was severely angled upward, like someone was reaching."

"And how tall do you calculate the killer would have been?"

"Objection, speculation," said the prosecutor.

The judge allowed the defense to proceed, warning once more that he would have irrelevant testimony stricken from the record.

"It is my opinion that Dr. Farquar's murderer was between five feet and five feet two inches tall. No more than that."

"And how tall would you say Mr. Jackson is?"

"At least six foot two," answered the doctor.

The courtroom was really buzzing now.

The judge hammered his gavel and called for order.

"So, Dr. Boone," said Mr. Dulany, "in your professional opinion, Dr. Farquar died of a stab wound from the back of the right side of his neck that cut his carotid artery."

"That is correct."

"And that the perpetrator was weaker and shorter than Dr. Farquar?"

"That is correct."

"And weaker and shorter that Mr. Jackson?"

"That is correct."

"I have no further questions for this witness, your honor," said Mr. Dulany. He said, "Your witness," turning to the prosecutor.

The cross-examination lasted over an hour. The prosecutors tried their best to find holes in the doctor's testimony, but he didn't flinch. I was proud of him. Mickey beamed.

When he was finished, Dr. Boone walked straight up the aisle and out the door. He didn't look at anybody. I followed him out.

I found him sitting on the steps with his head in his hands, shaking like a leaf.

"You did great, Dr. Boone," I said.

"I hope so," he said. "I hope it was enough. I'm just praying those men will do the right thing. You never know what will happen when men's minds are made up."

"Why didn't you tell us you were working on this case?"

"It was confidential. I wasn't supposed to talk about it. I've known George Dulany since he was a little boy. He knew I lived nearby and asked me to investigate, and I agreed. I told him I knew Mr. Jackson's son and there might be a conflict, but he said we'd take that chance."

Then he said, "I think I'll go home now, I'm pretty worn out. See you tomorrow?"

"OK. See you tomorrow."

The Jacksons went home with us that afternoon. They had been getting a lot of bad phone calls and ugly letters, and my folks thought it would be better if they stayed with us the night before closing arguments. Mrs. Jackson wouldn't quit talking about Dr. Boone. She said she wanted to go up to his house and give him a big, fat kiss.

Mickey stayed in my room. We talked a long time before going to sleep. We were feeling pretty good after today and the doctor's testimony. I don't know about Mickey, but I slept OK.

Final Arguments

I woke up Mickey early. We dressed and went in the kitchen to ask Daddy what the newspaper had to say. The headline read:

FINAL ARGUMENTS TODAY
IN CAPITAL MURDER TRIAL
Medical Opinions Conflict

Daddy said the prosecuting attorney's examiner's opinion wasn't anything like Dr. Boone's. It didn't seem nearly as thorough. That examiner just said Dr. Farquar had died of numerous stab wounds to the back side. Daddy said it was obvious that this guy wasn't as qualified as Dr. Boone and he hoped that made a difference. Daddy also admitted that he was prejudiced.

"What do you mean?" Mickey asked. He thought everything looked so good the day before.

Daddy said, "Mickey, when you're dealing with people, you never know what to expect. You'd like to think that those twelve men up there in the jury booth see everything with an open and honest eye. I hope that's true today. I'm sure praying that Mr. Dulany has all the right words for your papa."

"And I'm praying for that JURY!" said Mama as she came in the kitchen to fix us all breakfast.

Mrs. Jackson came in right after that and jumped in helping Mama. She was all smiles and laughter. You'd never know her husband's life was on the line that day. She was pure optimism. You could sure tell where Mickey got his attitude.

While the pancakes and bacon smelled up the room, Daddy said, "Why don't you boys stay here today? There won't be anything for you to do in Waco but wait. You'll find out what happened soon enough."

That was fine with me and fine with Mickey. We could go down to the creek or something. Maybe we could go fishing or get a ball game up. We'd probably do all of that.

Instead, we went to Dr. Boone's. We had too many questions. We said we'd pretend we wanted to work on birdhouses.

I knocked on the door. When the doctor answered, he told us to go on back to the workshop and he'd be out in a little bit. We knew what to do.

We slid the big door open and turned on the light. Dr. Boone had cut out a lot of pieces, so we started nailing birdhouses together. We weren't sure how many he needed for the next craft sale.

Mickey asked, "When's the next sale?"

"Fourth of July."

When the doctor came out in his work clothes, Mickey blurted, "Dr. Boone, how did you know my papa was left-handed?"

He said, "Top, do you remember when I told you that the name Leonard Jackson sounded familiar?"

"Sure do. It was the day the news came out."

"It finally came to me."

He continued, "You know what a big baseball fan I am. Back in the late forties, I started following the Fort Worth Cats Double A Club. This was after I'd lost my family and needed a distraction. The drive to Fort Worth was long, but they had a pitcher from my hometown of Pinson, Alabama, named Eddie Chandler. He was pretty good, and I knew his family. The Cats were a Dodgers affiliate. Eddie spent 1947 playing for Brooklyn. He started one game in the big leagues and relieved the rest of the time. I even have an autographed Eddie Chandler Nokona glove in the closet. There, I've gotten off track. You know how I get when we start talking baseball."

Mickey said, "Yeah, about Papa."

"You know he played for the Cats, don't you?" quizzed the doctor.

"I knew he played baseball, but he never talked about it much. Was he any good?"

Doctor Boone smiled and nodded. "He was very good. I kept following the Cats after Eddie quit playing and after baseball integrated. Your papa played first base. That's how I knew he was left-handed. He pitched some, too. He could run, hit, steal. He could do it all. I remember thinking he could have made it to the big leagues someday."

"What do you think kept him from it?"

"Well," said Dr. Boone, raising his eyebrows and looking straight at Mickey with a smile, "I think he probably met a pretty girl and started thinking about having a wife and family. That happens to a lot of men."

Mickey scrunched his face.

Then he said, "You know, if I were you boys on a pretty morning like this, instead of doing manual labor, I'd want to be fishing. Why don't you grab those poles on the wall and go down to the fishing hole behind my house? You can dig up some worms in the flower bed."

That sounded like a good invitation to us.

"Then you can go swimming later when it's hotter than all git out."

Mickey pulled the fishing poles off the wall, and I picked up the shovel and found a can for the worms.

We caught a few perch and threw them back. It was fun. Then Mickey caught a catfish that I supposed would have weighed a couple of pounds. That guy had all the luck. We showed the catfish to the doctor, and he said that if we cleaned it, he would fry it up for lunch. He had some cornmeal. That sounded good.

We spent the rest of the day at Dr. Boone's. We didn't intend to; it just worked out that way. Fishing and swimming on a hot day was hard to beat and much better than sitting and baking on the hard steps of the McClennan County Courthouse.

We started walking back to our house about the time my folks should be getting home. On the way, we passed the Ellises' house. Joe was out front wearing his glove.

"Hi, guys," said Joe, "what are y'all up to?"

"Just going home," I said; "how about you?"

"I've been to baseball practice, and now I'm waiting for supper. Have you heard anything new?"

"No," I answered. Mickey was being quiet, not knowing how to take Joe. "We're going to see if my folks are back from Waco. Then we'll get a report."

Joe said, "My daddy sure was impressed with Dr. Boone yesterday. So was I. It was an eye-opener."

"That's good; we hope the jury thinks so, too."

"I'm sorry about Daddy. Sometimes, he can't help himself," said Joe, looking down at his glove.

"That's OK," I said; "we're just hoping for the best. See you later."

When we got to the house, nobody was home. It was almost seven before Daddy drove up the driveway. They had dropped Mickey's mama at her house for the night and then stopped at the Health Camp to pick up some Super Health Burgers for supper since it was so late. We got milkshakes, too. What a treat! They had also picked up Sis and Sammy on their way home. It was good to see them. Things seemed kind of normal for a change.

Mickey would spend another night with us, and we would take him home in the morning.

Sammy was sitting up now, and Mickey played with her while Mama set the table. I knew he was afraid to ask, so I asked for him.

"Daddy, how'd it go today?"

"It's hard to tell. The prosecutors did everything they could to convict Mickey's papa. They were trying real hard. They especially tried to tear up Dr. Boone's testimony. I'll have to give it to Mr. Dulany. He gave it all he had, and more. I think he really believed in this case."

"Of course he did," jumped in Mickey. "It's the truth."

"I know," said Daddy, "but truth and justice don't always hold sway."

I didn't know what that meant and neither did Mickey.

"How did the jury look?" I asked.

Daddy didn't know what I meant, so we were even.

"I kept looking at the jury yesterday, and they didn't give a clue as to what they were thinking."

Daddy said he never thought to even look at them. Mama didn't, either.

"Did the crowd get noisy?" I asked. "It sure did yesterday."

"Well, it did when Dr. Farquar's wife got up and left during Mr. Dulany's rehash of Dr. Boone's testimony. She ran out crying and very upset. The guards escorted the little lady outside."

"What now?" Mickey asked.

"We'll just have to wait on the jury," Daddy said. "It could take a couple of days or longer. I don't know which would be best."

Mama had our plates on the table. She said, "Eat up."

Daddy said, "Sit down, Ruth; you forgot about saying grace."

She said, "Sorry, Bobby, I wasn't thinking. My stomach was."

We bowed our heads and we all held hands. Daddy said, "Dear Lord, thank you for your many blessings and your many gifts. Thank you for the food you've placed before us. This night, please be with those making hard decisions. Please be with the Jackson family, the Farquar family, and all the other families affected by these terrible events. May your will be done in all things. In Christ's name we pray. Amen."

Then Daddy looked at us and said with a smile, "Eat up."

Mickey didn't know what to say, so he didn't say anything. He just ate and played with Sammy. He poked Sis some. She liked that.

I didn't want to ask Daddy or Mama any more questions about the trial, and I could tell they didn't want to talk about it in front of Mickey. It was Thursday night, so, after supper, Mickey and I watched *Star Trek*. We loved that show. Dr. Spock was really cool.

When we went to bed, Mickey asked me what I thought.

I said, "I think your papa got caught in a bad situation, and I hope he doesn't have to suffer any more for it. He's spent enough time in jail without cause, just because your family couldn't afford bail. I hope the jury does the right thing. I know you do."

"You bet I do!"

We were dog-tired and had to get up early again.

I said, "Good night, Mickey."

He said, "Live long and prosper." He gave me the Vulcan peace sign with his middle fingers spread apart.

"You're a nut," I said as I rolled over in bed. I dreamed about being transported to other places. That was a good night's sleep.

Verdict

It was a week later, and the jury still hadn't reached a decision. I hadn't seen Mickey. He and his mom were staying close to home. The threats, phone calls, and hate mail had pretty much stopped. Mama called Mrs. Jackson every day to see how they were doing. She always let me talk to Mickey then. He wasn't going to the Boys' Club, just staying around the house and watching TV.

Our last game of the regular season was on Tuesday night. It was John's Farm-acy against the Milk Barn for the City Championship. CoachDaddy and Dr. Boone were down the right field line, as usual. There was one out in the bottom of the sixth, and we were tied at two. Alan Carpenter stood on second base, and I was up. A base hit would win it for us. We were playing at Optimist Field. That right field fence was really close. I tried not to think about that.

Ralph Reagan was pitching for the Milk Barn. He was eleven, but he was their best pitcher. We had the two best teams in the league. Ralph would make All-Stars, for sure. He threw me to full count. All fastballs. I fouled off three or four. I can't remember how many. Full count with the game on the line. This sounded familiar.

I heard Mama and Nana screaming, "Come on, Topper!"

I stepped out, rubbed up my bat, and looked at coach. Swing away. OK! I looked at CoachDaddy. He nodded.

Ralph brought the hard, high cheese. Swinging strike three. I just shook my head and went back to the dugout.

Thank goodness Jimmy James came up with a nice double to left field on the next pitch to win the game. Coach Blaine was beside himself. We were all jumping up and down like a bunch of nuts. You would've thought we'd won the World Series.

After the game, we all went to the Milk Barn for milkshakes.

Back at home, Mama let me call Mickey and tell him the news.

"How're you doing?" I asked.

"Pretty good," he said. "Just waiting."

"Maybe Daddy or Butch can bring you over for a day or two."

"I don't know," he said; "Mom wants me to stay close in case something happens."

"I see."

We talked a little more about other things. Mickey sounded all right, just anxious. That was understandable.

When we finished, Mama talked to Mrs. Jackson for a while.

They announced All-Stars on Thursday. I made it again. Coach Blaine was going to be the manager since we won the championship. That was good. Practices would start on Saturday morning.

On Friday morning, the *News-Tribune* headline said:

JURY IN CAPITAL MURDER TRIAL TO DELIVER VERDICT THIS A.M.

Daddy saw that and started scrambling.

"Ruth, get the kids ready; we need to go. The jury's announcing the verdict, and we need to be there."

All of us ran around, pulling on clothes, combing hair, and tugging on shoes. We dropped Sis and Sammy off at Nana's and headed straight to the courthouse.

On the way to Waco, Daddy repeated his lecture about "shadow of a doubt." He'd been going over and over this with me. How each one of the jury members had to find Mr. Jackson guilty based on the evidence presented "beyond a shadow of a doubt." Daddy just knew there had to be enough doubt to save Mr. Jackson. But, then, he would turn around and say, "But you never know about people." Life is confusing, isn't it? I decided then it was confusing for grown-ups, too.

I knew Mickey would show up at the courthouse sooner or later, and, sure enough, he was already there, waiting on the steps. He was dressed in his church clothes. I guess his mom wanted him to look nice for some reason. Mickey told us that Mr. Dulany had called them early that morning to tell them what was going on and to get ready. Mama gave him a big hug. Daddy shook his hand. They went inside.

I said, "Hey."

Mickey said, "Hey." He gave me the Vulcan peace sign. "Did you watch last night?" he asked.

"Yeah, it was good. I keep hearing they're going to cancel the show."

He said, "I hope not. It's my favorite show."

"Mine, too."

We talked like that for a while and sat on the steps and waited. One of the guards came out and asked if we needed some water or anything. We told him we were fine.

Around eleven o'clock, the courthouse doors opened and people started pouring out. Newspaper reporters, cameramen, people from the TV stations. Everybody was yelling, trying to talk above each other. It was chaos. After a while, Mama and Daddy found us and led us away from the crowd.

We were asking, "What happened?" but Daddy couldn't hear us for all the noise.

All he could say was, "Come on!"

When we reached the street curb, Mama was there, waiting. She was out of breath.

We asked again, "What happened?"

"Just a second," Daddy said and pointed toward the courthouse.

Just then, we saw Mr. Dulany coming down the steps with Mr. and Mrs. Jackson. Mr. Jackson wasn't wearing handcuffs. Photographers were taking pictures, and reporters were trying to talk to them. Mr. Dulany stopped and said something. We couldn't hear what it was. All we knew was that the Jacksons were hugging and smiling.

"Does this mean that my papa is a free man, that he's innocent?" asked Mickey.

"He's free right now," said Daddy. He continued, "I wish it were clearer cut."

"What do you mean?" We both had funny looks on our faces.

"The judge declared a hung jury," Daddy told us.

"What does that mean?" we asked together.

"It means that the jury couldn't agree on a verdict. After a solid week of deliberation, the vote was nine to acquit and three to convict, and neither side was giving in. They convinced the judge of that, and he let them go home."

"What now?" asked Mickey.

"Your Papa's a free man under the jurisdiction of the court until the prosecuting attorney decides whether or not he wants a retrial. Based on the weight of the vote, I would hope not."

"How long does that take?" Mickey looked worried again.

"That, I don't know. Just be glad your papa's going to be home tonight. I know your mom is. Now, you boys get in the car. I told Mrs. Jackson we'd bring Mickey home."

On the way to Mickey's house, Daddy talked up the justice system and the basic goodness of most people and how he believed things worked out OK in this old world.

When Mickey got out of the car, he was beaming so bright I thought his smile would put my eyes out.

Back in Tonkaway, I decided to head up to the doctor's and tell him the news. I didn't understand it all, but he would.

"That doesn't surprise me," said Dr. Boone, "but it's too bad Mr. Jackson has to wait a little longer to be fully exonerated. I hope I don't have to testify again. That was like juggling chainsaws for me. I was a nervous wreck."

"You sure didn't show it."

"It was all inside. You should have seen me when I got home. I just collapsed on the couch."

Then he told me he had a couple of birdhouses in the shop that needed painting if I wanted to do that.

I said I would.

At home that night, I lay awake thinking about those three "knuckleheads," as Daddy called them. How could anyone listen to Dr. Boone's testimony and not have a shadow of a doubt? It was beyond my sixth-grade mind. Anyway, Mr. Jackson was home and Mickey was smiling, so I slept just fine.

19

Strange World

It had been another week, and the prosecuting attorney still hadn't made a decision. Baylor had let Mr. Jackson go back to work. The Jacksons were acting like everything was normal. We had our first All-Star game on Thursday night, so I missed *Star Trek* again. We played Crawford and won eight to one. I started at first base and hit another home run. I didn't need short fences any more. After we went to the Milk Barn for milkshakes, Mama let me call Mickey.

"How was the game?" he asked.

"We won. How was *Star Trek*?"

"It was good. It was about these little hamsters called tribbles that kept multiplying. It was kind of funny, for a change."

"Maybe I'll see the rerun." I said.

We didn't have a lot more to talk about. I told him I'd try to come over to the Boys' Club on Saturday if baseball didn't interfere. We would play Oglesby on Monday. If we won that game, we'd play the winner of the Midway-Wood-way game for the Area Championship on Thursday and go to Houston after that.

Friday morning's paper had an interesting headline. All it said was:

Waco Police Reopen Investigation
Prosecutor Waits on Decision

"What does this mean?" I asked Daddy as he sipped his coffee.

"I don't know. It seems they're being pretty tight-lipped about what they are doing."

After breakfast, I went across the street and mowed the Alexanders' yard and collected my five dollars. Then I went up to Dr. Boone's to see if he had read the *News-Tribune* yet.

His paper was still in the mailbox, so I took it to the house and knocked on the door. When he answered, I just opened it up and showed him the headline. He raised his eyebrows, his ears went back, and the corners of his lips went down.

He went, "Hmmmm. Interesting."

"What do you think?" I was sure curious about what this all meant.

"Let me read the rest of this, and I'll tell you."

He studied the story for a minute, took off his glasses, rubbed his eyes, put his glasses back on, looked at me, looked away, and looked back at me. I guess he was thinking.

Finally, he said, "My best guess is they might have another suspect and they don't want to tip their hand. The police investigators probably wish the news people never got wind of this, but they had to find out. I'll bet they started investigating whoever or whomever it is as soon as the trial was over, if not before."

"Do you think they're looking for somebody shorter and weaker than Mr. Jackson and Dr. Farquar?"

"I would hope so."

Then he just wanted to talk about last night's game. He said he was impressed that I had pulled an outside pitch over the right field fence. He said it reminded him of something left-handed Leonard Jackson would do for the Fort Worth Cats. I thought he was trying to build me up.

He let me go to the barn and work on birdhouses for a while before walking home. We had All-Star practice at five, and Coach told us not to swim and to take naps. I hadn't been told to take a nap since kindergarten.

On Monday night, we had a close game against Oglesby. We won five to four. I hit third in the lineup. Rex Johnson batted cleanup. Rex had grown a lot in the last year. At least he wasn't shaving. He turned out to be our best pitcher, too. He didn't start that night. Coach Blaine wanted to save him for the division championship game.

We scored what turned out to be the winning run in the top of the sixth, and I didn't even get to bat. I'd had a double in the second inning that scored a run, and I struck out in the fourth inning. High cheese, of course. Jimmy James pitched in the bottom of the sixth, and we held them. Coach Blaine had Rex warming up, just in case.

Tuesday morning's headline was awful. It said:

Prosecutor to Retry Murder Case
Investigation Ongoing

When Daddy showed that to me, I said, "I don't get it." There was a lot I didn't get in those days.

"I don't, either," said Daddy. "All I know is that they've taken Leonard back into custody."

I rode to Waco with Daddy, and he dropped me off at Mickey's on his way to work. He gave me five dollars and told me to buy Mickey lunch and he would pick me up at three. I could nap on the way home. Sure I would.

We spent the morning at the Boys' Club. I don't know what Mickey would have done without that place. Butch showed up, and we quizzed him to see if Mr. Pawelek knew anything, since he worked at the newspaper.

Butch said, "No, Pop's as confused as you are. We'll just have to see how this plays out."

We shot baskets for a while. Then we went into Mr. Garza's office to see what he thought.

Grown-ups were no help. Mickey and I decided to walk to Clark's and get cheeseburger baskets and Dr. Peppers.

On the way, I paid close attention to the cars that passed us. Most drove on by with no trouble. A couple of cars had folks who stared. A few actually waved or gave us the "hi" sign. There really were just a few knuckleheads, just like Daddy said. They were just noisy, but they had grown quiet lately.

When we got to Clark's, I went inside and ordered. I loved to watch them make burgers on the griddle. They kept balls of hamburger in a plastic shoebox, and when an order came through, the cook threw a ball on the griddle. Then he smashed it with a masonry trowel. I mean he smacked it. Right into a round burger. It was beautiful!

The same two men I'd heard talking about the trial before were there. They were in the same booth. They weren't as loud this time, but I could still hear them.

One said, "What if that n***** is innocent?"

The other said, "Somebody had to do it. Who else but the n*****?"

"I just cain't understand why they're still investigating if they think they've got the culprit. Three honest citizens had him dead to rights," said the first man.

"And nine bought all the excuses. Go figure," said the other.

Knuckleheads.

I tried to enjoy my cheeseburger, anyway. Mickey apparently loved his. The fries, too. Mama always said she was glad she didn't have to feed that boy all the time.

We washed everything down with our Dr. Peppers and walked back to Mickey's. There wasn't a whole lot left to say. We mainly talked about playing Midway Thursday night and me missing *Star Trek* again. I told Mickey that Daddy might bring him over to Tonkaway to spend the night and watch our game. He said that was a tough decision. Top, baseball, and Mama's cooking, or *Star Trek*. Laughing, he said he'd think about it.

I had a lousy practice that afternoon. Fielding and hitting, both. Coach Blaine asked me what was wrong. I said I didn't know. I think he knew. CoachDaddy showed up toward the end and saw how unmotivated I was.

He told me, "You'd better get your head on. This thing could drag out for a while again. Mickey's going to come over and make fun of you."

I don't know what kept me awake that night. Mr. Jackson being in jail or the idea of Mickey making fun of me.

20

Midway

The phone rang at seven a.m. Mama answered. It was Mickey.

He said, "Mrs. Parsley, I need to talk to Top."

She said, "OK, I'll have to get him out of bed."

Mama woke me up, and I picked up the phone.

Mickey told me, "Go get the newspaper and call me back." Then he hung up.

When I came in with the paper, I opened it up. Daddy was coming out of the shower, getting dressed.

"What's going on, Topper?" he asked.

"Look at this." I showed him the headline:

PROFESSOR'S WIFE ARRESTED
Leonard Jackson Released
Prosecutor Drops All Charges

"Daddy," I said, "I've asked this question a million times lately, but what does this mean?"

"It means that Mickey's papa has been exonerated. They can't try him again. Now they're going to try Mrs. Farquar."

I said, "You're kidding? She acted so upset at the trial."

Daddy started reading and said, "People can put on when they have to. From what I'm reading here, after Dr. Boone's testimony, the detectives started asking more questions around the Baylor campus. It turns out that Mrs. Farquar was seen leaving Pat Neff Hall the night of the murder in a big hurry. There are witnesses who came forward saying they tried to talk to her that night, but she wouldn't stop."

"Is that all?" I was excited.

"No, it seems that Mrs. Farquar had tried to cash in a $300,000 life insurance policy on Dr. Farquar. Apparently, she just assumed that Mr. Jackson would be found guilty and she was in the clear. Remember what I told you about knuckleheads?"

"All the time."

After breakfast, I kissed Mama and Sis and Sammy goodbye and headed up to Dr. Boone's. I must have been mighty giddy to have kissed Sis. The doctor's paper was in the mailbox, so I knew he hadn't heard the news.

When I went in and opened up the front page, his face glowed.

"Top," he said, "There is justice in God's world. Sometimes, it just takes a little longer than others. Our prayers have been answered. And there have been a lot of them."

"I know. And a lot of sleepless nights."

"Boys your age shouldn't have sleepless nights," he said.

"There's too much going on not to, sir," I said.

"I know what you mean. Thanks for coming up. Why don't you run back home? You've got a big game tonight."

It was a big game, and I felt great. I was almost skipping along when I passed the Ellises' house. Joe was mowing their yard. He turned the mower off and waved at me. We talked a minute.

"Did you hear about Mickey's Papa?" I asked.

"Yeah, Daddy told me." Joe shrugged. "I couldn't tell what he thought."

"What do you think?" I wanted to know.

"I think it's great. I'm happy for Mickey. I just wish Daddy wasn't the way he was. Maybe someday he'll come around. Don't you have a big game tonight?"

"Sure do."

Joe wasn't on All-Stars this year. He had to play in the Pony League because of his age. His pitching wasn't nearly as overpowering since the rubber stretched fifteen feet farther from the plate. He had to make quite an adjustment with his throwing. I would have to make the same adjustment the next year, which is why I had to enjoy that year while I could.

Leaving Joe's, I realized I'd forgotten to call Mickey back. When I did, he just said, "What took so long? I've been waiting."

"Sorry, I had to go tell Dr. Boone the news and forgot."

"Well, we're awfully happy in this house right now. Papa's bringing Mom and me to Tonkaway tonight to watch you play. You'd better come through."

"We will."

His last words were "Lay off the high cheese."

"OK," I said, "but you know I love it."

No, I didn't take a nap that afternoon. Who could have? I did show up at the game ready to play, though. It might be my last Little League game, and I didn't want it to end.

The game started. CoachDaddy was down the right field line with Dr. Boone. Mama had come early with Nana, Sis, and Sammy. She saved places for Mr. and Mrs. Jackson and Mickey. Mickey was holding Sammy and playing with her.

All of the Midway guys were big. They must have been held back for football. I'd have bet they had at least twelve pitchers.

Even though I'd had a crummy practice the day before, Coach Blaine had me batting cleanup. He said he could tell I was feeling pretty good. He was right.

The baseball looked like a cantaloupe. It was huge. I got a hit every time up. They were all singles, but they were hits.

Rex pitched a good game. He only gave up three runs after six innings. Unfortunately, we'd only scored two runs.

So there we were, the bottom of the sixth and down three to two. We had the top of the lineup coming up, but Rex grounded out to the shortstop. Alan Carpenter hit a single to left field. Jimmy James struck out on the high cheese.

That left it up to me. Down one run, a man on first, and two outs.

The first pitch was a wild pitch, and Alan went to second base. Now a base hit would tie it up.

Second pitch, ball outside. Third pitch, high, fast cheese. I swung and missed. Two balls, two strikes. I looked down at CoachDaddy. He grinned. I stepped out and rubbed up my Nellie Fox bat, as usual.

I fouled off the next three pitches. One went straight down the left field line. I thought Coach Blaine was going to catch it. The next one went back to the screen. I turned and looked at Mickey. He smiled and gave me the Vulcan peace sign. The next pitch was a pop-up over the screen. I watched as Cherry Ann caught it. She smiled and waved it at me.

OK, two balls, two strikes. Coach Blaine gave me the "swing away" sign. The pitcher brought the high cheese.

And I laid off it.

I look down at CoachDadddy and he smiled. Full count. Man on second. Down by one. Game on the line. Way back in the stands, I heard a voice saying, "Come on, Topknot!"

I dug in. The next pitch was a fastball right down the middle. It looked bigger than a cantaloupe. I swung, and it felt really good. I didn't watch it go out. I just knew, so I ran.

Goodbye, ball! Hello, Houston!

That night, I slept like a baby.

Coming Home

After over thirty years of medical practice in Dallas, it was time to come home. Tonkaway had always been home. Even though I'd only lived there for seven years, they were the most important years of my life. That's when I became who I am. Mama and Daddy are still there, although they are getting up in years. We'd been looking at nursing homes in Waco, but I have a tough time imagining them not living on their own.

I grew tired of the big-city rat race and decided to open up a small family practice here in my hometown. Dr. Gillespie's clinic closed down years ago, and there wasn't a real family doctor there anymore, just a franchise clinic. The income wouldn't be as good, but my wife, Paula, and I would be happy there. Our daughters, Riann and Reese, lived in Waco, so that would be convenient. These days, I might be flipping pancakes at the Rotary Club Pancake Breakfast or chasing rubber ducks down Tonkaway Creek on July the Fourth.

Paula and I bought Dr. Boone's old house on the creek and are fixing it up a little at a time. All of his tools were still in the barn. They just needed cleaning. Once the house is finished, I'll probably start making birdhouses again. Maybe we'll sell them at the Memorial Day Craft Fair.

Dr. Boone has been dead for twenty years now. It's hard to believe. He lived a great life, whether he knew it or not. He touched a lot of lives, despite his sorrows.

It turns out that this old house was built by a Texas Ranger named Josiah Woodshank in the early 1900s. He raised fourteen children here. One of his sons became a Texas state representative. Another son tended bar in Tonkaway and probably knew Shaky Man in his bad days. The Texas State Historical Commission wants to make this house an official historical site with a plaque and all. Not bad for an old place little kids used to run from, screaming.

I'm spending a lot of time clearing brush, especially along the creek bed. I hate to admit that I occasionally look for webbed tracks in the mud. The rest of the time, I'm scraping, painting, or polishing doorknobs.

The city of Tonkaway has invested a lot of money and energy making Tonkaway into an attraction for tourists and shoppers. The Phillipses' old house is now a bed and breakfast.

Joe Ellis quit growing in the ninth grade. Needless to say, he never made it to the pros. He did get to play quarterback for the Tonkaway Tigers, though. His arm was still strong. He was just a little short for seeing over the linemen. He went to Tarleton State on a scholarship but didn't get to play very much. He's back in Tonkaway, running an insurance agency.

I kept growing. I'm about six foot two now. I weighed 170 pounds in High School. That was pretty big for Tonkaway, so I played fullback and linebacker. I wasn't that good, but I loved it. CoachDaddy was proud. He would watch our games from the end zone and chew on his cigar. He said he could see the holes open up better down there. We won district our senior year. That was because the junior and sophomore classes were so good.

Mickey Jackson? After making All-State at Waco's Carver High, he went on to play football at SMU, where he was a second-team All-American. Then he spent ten years with the Dallas Cowboys. He never left Texas. He was best man at our wedding. We are still as close as brothers. He is also the mayor of Waco. A lot of people think he will be the Governor of Texas someday. I learned a long time ago not to put anything past him. He still makes me laugh. And we've both lived long and prospered.

We've raised four children and have six grandchildren. Our boys live in the Dallas area. The grandkids love to come see Nanny and Paw-Paw and play along Tonkaway Creek. They especially love the stories about our beloved Shaky Man. Sometimes, at night, they get out their flashlights and make me tell them about the Green Ghost of Tonkaway Creek. I let them paint birdhouses, too.

And the mayor of Tonkaway? His name is Joe Ellis. Go figure.

We have great days ahead and a good bed to sleep in, where I sleep mighty fine every night.

About the Author

Shaky Man is Mark S. Parker's first published novel for young people. He is a graduate of Texas A&M University, and he has been involved in the oil business for over thirty years. Writing has always been a pleasant pastime for him, but he started taking children's fiction seriously with the arrival of his five grandchildren. They are his muse. Mark and his wife Ann live in Midland, Texas, where they raised their four children.